Litt~~le Wolf's~~

Big Book of Badness
and Daring Deeds

TWO
adventures in wun
big book from the
NUMBER 1 CUB!

Collins

An imprint of HarperCollinsPublishers

Also by Ian Whybrow and illustrated by Tony Ross
Little Wolf's Haunted Hall for Small Horrors
Little Wolf's Postbag
Little Wolf, Forest Detective

Little Wolf's Book of Badness was first published by Collins in 1995
Little Wolf's Diary of Daring Deeds was first published by Collins in 1996
First published in this omnibus edition by Collins in 2001

**Little Wolf's Book of Badness won the TSB Birmingham
Children's Book Award in 1996, and an U.K.R.A Book Award
for making a substantial contribution to children's literacy.**

Collins is an imprint of HarperCollinsPublishers Ltd,
77 – 85 Fulham Palace Road, Hammersmith, London W6 8JB

The HarperCollins Website address is www.**fire**and**water**.com
Little Wolf's website address is www.littlewolf.co.uk

1 3 5 7 9 8 6 4 2

Text copyright © Ian Whybrow 1995 and 1996
Illustrations copyright © Tony Ross 1995 and 1996

ISBN 0 00 712890 8

Printed and bound in Great Britain by
Omnia Books Limited, Glasgow.

Little Wolf's

Book of Badness

Ian Whybrow
Illustrated by Tony Ross

The Lair, Murkshire

Dear Bigbad

I have had no reply to my many letters to you. I therefore have no choice but to send this one by the paw of my eldest cub, Little Wolf. I want you to be his teacher.

Little is a bad boy at heart, I am sure, but he is worryingly well-behaved at the moment. He has been far too nice to Smellybreff, his baby brother, and only yesterday he went to bed early without being growled at. His mother and I think that it is time he left the Lair and had some adventures. We want him to go to Cunning College to learn his 9 Rules of Badness, and earn a BAD badge, just as you and I did long ago at Brutal Hall.

We are at our wits' end. You are our only hope. We rely on you to make a beast of Little Wolf.

Your anxious brother,

Gripper

Dear Mum and Dad,

Please please PLEEEEEZ let me come home. I have been walking and walking all day, and guess how far? Not even ten miles, I bet. I have not even reached Lonesome Lake yet. You know I hate going on adventures. So why do I have to go hundreds of miles to Uncle Bigbad's school in the middle of a dark damp forest?

You say you do not get on in life these days without a BAD badge. But I know loads of really bad wolves who never went to school. Ever. Like my cousin Yeller for one. I know you want me to be wild and wicked like Dad, but why do I have to go so far away? Just what is so wonderful about Cunning College in Frettnin Forest? And what is so brilliant

7

about having Uncle Bigbad as a teacher? Is it all because Dad went to Brutal Hall and they made him a prefect and he got a silver BAD badge when he left? I bet it is.

There is another four days' walk, maybe more to Frettnin Forest. Let me come back and learn to be bad at home. PLEE-EE-EEZ!!!

Your number 1 cub,

Little Wolf

PS Don't forget to say Hello baby bruv to Smellybreff and tell him not to touch any of my things.

Dear Mum and Dad,

I am a bit lost.

I think I have come to Lonesome Lake just where the River Rover runs up to it. I used Dad's map as a tablecloth for my picnic lunch. Now it is hard to tell if you have come to a river or a bit of bacon rind.

I have not had word from you to return home, so I must continue on this stupid long journey, even though I might never find Uncle Bigbad. He never answers Dad's letters. Maybe Cunning College is closed, and he has moved from Frettnin Forest. Anyway, how will I know I have found him when I do?

BIGBAD

HUGE REWARD

I have got the Wanted poster that you gave me, but it is years old. Maybe he has changed. What will he look like now? Too scary, I bet!

Just now the sun fell in the water. I did not like it. Now the moon has come up and I can just see my pen and paper but I wish it was brighter. My tent is stupid. It falls down all the time, so I have curled up in my rucksack. Camping is my worst thing, and maps too. I am frozz, I am hopeless.

Yours tiredoutly,

Little Wolf

Dear Mum and Dad,

I woke up this morning feeling a bit tickly
with ants in my rucksack. They were small
but plenty of them, and quite tasty for breakfast. Then I was more cheery. I started
walking soon after the sun jumped out.
It was hiding behind a hill.

3 hours later.

I have stopped now for a rest and
one of Mum's rabbit rolls. Yum
yum, only 25 left, worse luck. Shall
probably starve... You know I am a
hopeless hunter.

You just think I am a goody-goody, I bet.
Is that the reason why I have to go away for
badness lessons? But I told you I only
cleaned my teeth last week for a joke.
And brushing my fur, and going to bed early,

that was just to trick you! You ask my cousin
Yeller, it was his idea. He said let's *pretend*
being good. I just said OK. So I pretended.
Then you were s'posed to say, "Oh no, Little
Wolf has gone barmy." Then I was s'posed
to say, "Arr Harr, tricked you, I am a bad
boy really." But no, you would not listen,
you did not understand. You said I must go
to Cunning College, I must live in Frettnin
Forest until I get my BAD badge and learn
Uncle Bigbad's 9 Rules of Badness.

I bet you won't make Smellybreff leave
home when he is my age. You will just say,
"Oh yes, my darling baby pet. You stay here
safe with us and watch telly all you want."
And what about Yeller? I 'spect you think he
is a small bad wolf but no. You do not see
him doing good things like I do. Like the
kite he made for me to take with me, with
yellow wolf-eyes painted on it. And sometimes he says pardon when he burps, too.
Bet his mum and dad are nice and do not
send him to school in a faraway forest.

Yours fedduply,
Little Wolf

Dear Mum and Dad,

Aaah, the hunters got me in Lonesome Woods, urg.

Only kidding, I am all right really. Had you worried though, eh?

Walked miles today and have got to Spring Valley, but still a long long way to go. Have eaten most of Mum's rabbit rolls already, boo, shame. I can smell your present for Uncle Bigbad, lots of lovely mice pies. Yum, yes please, scoff scoff (not really).

I wonder if Uncle is as greedy as you said. Hope he is not ~~crool~~ cruel, I am only small. That reminds me. Tell my baby bruv Smellybreff not to chew my teddy bear or I will chew him back.

Dad's map is a bit wrong because there is no big black monster between Lonesome Woods and Murky Mountains. I looked and looked but it is only trees here. Off to Roaring River tomorrow.

Love from

Little Wolf

PS. Oh dear, it was not a big black monster on the map. It was a squashed ant, sorry.

Dear Mum and Dad,

I am writing this
under a bridge at a
town called Roaring
River. This makes six
bridges I have crossed
on my journey, and
still not even in
Beastshire yet. I am
sure it is much much
further to Frettnin
Forest than Dad said.

Spent last night in a bus shelter. Quite
warm and unscary, with my torch switched
on going flash. Mum always says yellow eyes
are friends with the dark. True, but it is still
nice to have a torch when you are a small
loner.

Roaring River is too big, not a good place to wake up. There are so many human people here you would not believe. It is not safe for cubs.

Yours watchingly,

Little

Dear Mum and Dad,

Spent the day in Roaring River. I like the cars, they are nice and smelly and good growlers. And buses are best of all. They go FSSSHHH when they stop and the people line up and get inside them. It is funny, just like Dad eating sausages.

This morning I wanted to try being a sausage. So I got in a line behind a large woman at the bus stop. Then guess what, she hit me with her shopping just for wearing a fur coat. She said, "Take that for animal rights." I said, "Stop, I *am* an animal!" She said, "What sort?", so I told her and she ran off screaming, har har.

Her shopping was quite tasty except some white powdery stuff in a box. It made your tongue go bubbly . . .

Yours spittily,

Little Wolf

Dear Mum and Dad,

I was glad to leave Roaring River. Feel a bit better after good gargle in a stream, and all the nasty froth spat out at last.

Got to Crowfeet Crossroads by noon. Nice houses here, but not as nice as our smelly cave. Did not see any people, only a post box to post this.

I had a think today. Do you know what? Everybody else thinks I am bad, even if you think I am a Goodie-4-Paws. Remember when Mum was asleep that time and I nipped off her whiskers with the claw clippers? And what

about when I glued Smellybreff's tail to his
high chair? So whyo Y do I have to make
this stupid long journey?

Just now I thought I heard Yeller calling
me. It was only a train howling in the valley.
I am going now up the steep and wiggly path
through the Murky Mountains. It looks
VERY dangerous. Hope you are satisfied.

Farewell from

L Wolf

Dear M and D,

I had some big shocks today.

You did not say about how
cold it gets up in the mountains.
You have to climb up and up
above Crowfeet Crossroads.
Sometimes you are up so high
that nothing grows, not even
trees. And the ice makes your
feet slip. Two times I nearly
skidded right over the edge of
the path. It was terrible. When
I peeped over, the houses down below
looked small as sparrow nests.

Then I got lost. I followed one thin path.
It just went round and round and came
back where I started. So I wrote TRICK

PATH in big letters on a rock for the next
traveller. And off I went fedduply.

Just before dark I found the edge of
Murkshire. I felt sleepy and wanted to lie
down. My breath was white clouds. Then I
saw a deep dark tunnel going into a mountain wall and a sign above the entrance. It
said

My fur started jumping up all along my back. But I did not want to stay in the open and freeze. So big breath and in I went, running, running. I shouted, "Can't scare me. Yellow eyes are friends with the dark!" Then guess what! My words shouted back – only louder and growlier! I ran and ran with my puff hot in my throat. I had just enough puff to get to the end. It was the best feeling ever to be in the open, looking at the moon shining down. It was shining on the village of Borderlands Market.

And that was how I got here.
Just.

Can't keep awake. More tomorrow.

Dear Mum and Dad,

Guess who woke me up
this morning? I will
give you a clue. He
has got sharp eyes, a
pointy face, red bristly
fur and a smell like
pepper.

I was all curled up under a small cart near
a street light in the market square – zzzz –
fast asleep. All of a suddenly, I felt hot breath
in my ear and this voice saying, "My boy!" I
jumped up and banged my head. I tried to
run but strong paws held me down and then
I yelled, "Ooo-er, a fox!"

The fox said, "Mister Twister is my name.
You are camping under my stall." I said,
"Whoops, sorry, Mister Twister." He said,
"Do not worry yourself, my boy. There will
be no charge. For now. But then, something tells me that you are a keen young
chappie who is eager to assist me with my
work today."

I did not know how to say no to him.
More later.

Yours stuckly,

Little

Dear Mum and Dad,

Yesterday I did work in the market for Mister Twister. He sells dizgizzes (cannot spell it). My job was putting on false beards, masks, sheep's clothing, etc. and walking up and down saying, "Hey, guess what I am?" It was quite good fun dressing up, and loads of people stopped to buy things.

A small mouse came up to me and he said, "I am lonely. Can you sell me something to help me make friends?" I said, "Yes, I can. Here are some tie-on wings. Wear these and stand on your head. Then loads of bats will come and play with you." And guess what?

He bought 2 pairs!

And my best thing was finding something for a stoat to wear to a fancy dress ball. I sold him half a coconut and told him to shave all his fur off. Then he could go as a tortoise! He was so pleased he said I could keep the change.

I like being a market worker.

Yours richly,

Little

Dear Mum and Dad,

Mister Twister said I was a good worker and would I stay? I wanted to but I told him I had to go to Cunning College and study for my BAD badge. "You amaze me!" he said, and his sharp eyes went wide, and his red fur went even more bristly. "Do you mean to tell me that you are going to Cunning College in Frettnin Forest?"

I said, "Yes, do you know it?"

He said, "My boy, I was a teacher in that school many a full moon ago! Your uncle and I used to be partners! Can you really be the nephew of that nasty mean bad horrid crook?"

I said a proud "Yes".

The fox told me more. He and Uncle Bigbad met ages ago in Broken Tooth Caves when they were both hiding from the police. Uncle had the idea to stay out of sight in Frettnin Forest and start a school for bad beasts. He promised Mister Twister that if he worked hard, teaching the naughty pupils everything he knew, he would soon be rich.

Mister Twister said, "My boy, it was dreadful. The pupils never gave me a moment's peace! They were most awfully sly and squirmy, all those little skunks and stoats and rattlesnakes and cubs! How they got on my nerves, those spoilt little brutes! And what a fuss their horrid parents made, always wanting to know when their ghastly off-spring would be getting their BAD badges! They quite wore me out. But when I asked your uncle for some money, just enough to allow me to take a short holiday, he threat-ened to eat me!"

I said, "What did he say?"

Mister Twister said, "He told me to get

out and he said that if I ever put a paw in his school again, he would boil my bones and serve me up as soup."

I said, "Oo-er!"

The fox said, "So you see, your uncle is a miser and a cheat. He has bags of money hidden away but he will not part with a penny of it. You would be unwise, my boy, to leave Borderlands Market. What is more, Frettnin Forest is a SHOCKING place, dismal, dark and lonely. Your Uncle Bigbad is dangerous. He has a terrible temper. In short, he is Mister Mean. My strong advice to you, my boy, is STAY AWAY FROM CUNNING COLLEGE!"

I said, "Yikes, you have got a point!"

Yours having a good think,

LW

Dear Dum and Mad,

I am a bit confused and bothered. Mister Twister wants me to stay with him for ever and be his dresser-upper. Sometimes I think Oh yes, nice idea because one day I could have a stall of my own. Next thing, I think Yes, but what about learning the 9 Rules of Badness? If I do not, how will I get a BAD badge and keep up the good name of Wolf?

But Mister Twister has got me worried about Uncle. I mean, about boiling him up as soup. If he is going to make soup out of his large friend, what will he make out of a small nephew he has never met? Will I be his special pupil or just a sausage in a sandwich?

Yours nervously,

Little

Dear Mum and Dad,

I have decided. I am going on. I think I like adventures now. (A bit, anyway.) Tell Smells and Yeller for me. It will be a good shock for them.

I slipped away from Borderlands Market very early before Mister Twister came and talked softly to me. I did not trust his voice. I have still got the bonnet he gave me for dressing up as an old lady. It might come in handy.

Borderlands Market and the mountains are far behind me now. Today was my longest walk ever. One good thing, the land was flat, but no shade for miles and miles. On the map, it is called The Parching Plain and now I know why. The track was dusty and the sun was hot. I was longing for a stream to

splash my tongue in but no luck. I wished
I had brought a snowball from the mountains
to lick.

In the afternoon, some big birds came, big
as planes. They glided round and round.
The slower I walked, the lower the birds flew.
About 4 o'clock one came close enough to
show his hooked beak and claws.

Then I remembered Yeller's present, my
kite with the yellow wolf-eyes painted on.
I had to stop to get it out of my rucksack
and fix it together. Now the birds came so
low I could see their shadows flick on the
stones near me. I howled to make them stay
back and then I was ready.

I tugged the string and the kite FLEW up.
I flipped and flapped it right in their ugly
faces. You should have seen them scatter! It
was like tadpoles in a pond when you plop in
a pebble!

Don't forget to tell Yeller. I kept his kite
flying right across The Parching Plain and

not one bird bothered me again.

    I am posting this just on the edge of
Frettnin Forest. I have not gone in yet but
tomorrow I will have to, worse luck. Oo-er.
It looks darker in there than the Borderlands
tunnel.

    Good thing I can whistle, eh?

    Yours chinupply,

Little W

Dear Mum and Dad,

I have arrived. It took me all day what with the paths so overgrown. But I have found Uncle's school at last. The fox was right. This IS the shockingest, dismalest darkest part of the forest.

Much too late to ring the bell. If I wake up Uncle now he is sure to eat me.

I have tried putting up my tent but no good. So I have made a small lair in a bush in the college garden, OK but a bit prickly.

Oh no, now it is drizzling here! Sorry about the smudges. I wish I was curled up under my nice dry rock at home.

Talk about spooky. So overgrown, with

35

eyes and croaks and squeaks everywhere!
Good thing I have got my torch. I am holding it in my mouth to see what I am writing.
Also, I can point it and light up a sign by the
door of the schoolhouse from here. It says

CUNNING COLLEGE.
BADGES AWARDED FOR
WICKED WAYS
DIRTY DEEDS
& BAD HABITS.

Gosh, sorry about that. Something
went WOO, made me jump. This is SO
scary, it stands your fur up.

Not sure when I will find post box but I
just want to say something. OK, I did teach
my little bruv I Love Little Pussy. And
Christopher Robin is Saying His Prayers
with actions, I admit that. But that was just
tricks, honest. You know I am not really
nice and polite. I do not usually brush my

teeth and fur either. You ask Yeller. I just hope Uncle isn't too cruel. I do not want to get boiled.

This could be my last letter.

Ever.

And it will be all your fault.

Yours damply,

Master L Wolf

PS Smellybreff can have my ted but I promised Yeller my box of tricks.

Dear Mum and Dad,

Guess what, not dead yet!

Woke up this morning so damp and frozz, I thought blow it, be brave, better be boiled than die of frozz. So I went ding ding on the bell.

Next thing, boom boom, big feet coming down the hall, loads of huff and puff. The door went *eeeeee-aaaaah* and there was Uncle Bigbad, all tall and thin and horrible. He is not like in the Wanted poster. His eyebrows are furry like caterpillars and they join in the middle. He is very fierce, and he has got great big red eyes and great big long yellow teeth and great big long streams of dribble dribbling down. He reminds me a bit of Dad, but hungrier. And he wears a great big gold BAD badge on his chest.

So I took a big breath to get steady but my voice went wobbly. "H-h-h-hello Uncle Badbiggy, I am your n-nephew L-Little Wolf. M-Mum and Dad sent me so you can t-teach me the 9 R-Rules of B-Badness."

He snarled his great big horrible snarl and he said in his great big horrible posh voice, "GGGRRR! BEGONE VILE BALL OF FLUFF! FLY AND FLEE OR I SHALL FETCH OUT THE VACUUM CLEANER AND HOOVER YOU UP OFF MY FRONT STEP!"

I said, "B-b-but I am your nephew, L-little W-Wolf. Didn't you get Dad's l-l-letters?"

He said, "GRRRR, I HAVE

CEASED TO RECEIVE LETTERS."

I said, "Why?"

He said, "BECAUSE THE POSTMEN
WILL NOT DELIVER. JUST BECAUSE I
DEVOURED 1 OR 2 OF THEM! IT IS
NOT FAIR, I AM ALWAYS STARVING
THESE DAYS! IN FACT, TALKING OF
FOOD, STAND STILL A MINUTE
WHILE I PUT SOME SALT AND
PEPPER ON YOU!"

I said, "Wait, Uncle, do not devour me,
try some rabbit rolls! I think I have 2 left.
They are a bit stale, sorry, but tastier than
me."

He said, "GRRRRR, GIVE THEM TO
ME SWIFTLY, SWIFTLY!" Then he
grabbed them and banged the door in my
face, bang.

Gulp, I am coming home.

Yours trembly,

Littly

Dear Mum and Dad,

I started going back along the forest path, running, running. I felt misery – no BAD badge, no lessons, nothing. Then I thought, Oh no, the shame, what will Mum and Dad say if I go home now? Oh boo, now I will have to camp out for ever, which is my worst thing.

THEN. Ding, I had an idea, Mum's mice pies that she made for Uncle's present! I hid half the pies in a hollow tree. Then I turned round, and I went creep creep to the college again. The letter box was too small, so I went round the back and climbed on to the roof. I got 1 mice pie and tied it to a long string off my kite (good old Yeller!). Then I let it down the chimney.

Next thing, I heard Uncle say,

"SNIF SNUFF SNY!
I SMELL PIE!"

And then Uncle's great big long tongue went SLIP SLAP. You could hear him going mad looking for pies, crashing the furniture about. So I jiggled the string. All of a sudden WOOOOOF, gone! No more mice pie.

Next I let down a little note, it said

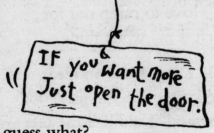

And guess what?

I am IN.

Your brainy boy,

L Wolf, ESQ

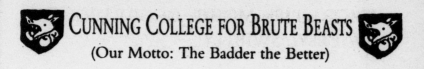

CUNNING COLLEGE FOR BRUTE BEASTS
(Our Motto: The Badder the Better)

Day 13

Dear Mum and Dad,

What a shock when I first went inside!
Cunning College was empty except for Uncle
and dust and cobwebs everywhere. Not one
pupil was left in the classroom. I said to
Uncle, "Where are all the pupils?"

CUNNING COLLEGE FOR BRUTE BEASTS

He said, "DEPARTED, SCATTERED!
I AM SO *FRIGHTFULLY* FRIGHTENING
THEY ALL FLED AND FLEW AWAY!
NOW GIVE ME MORE PIES,
GGRRRRR! SWIFTLY, SWIFTLY!"

What could I do? I gave him one and
down it went, GLUP. Then he said,

"MORE PIES, MORE! GGGRRRRR!
SWIFTLY! SWIFTLY!

So I said, "If I give you 1 more mice pie,
will you be my teacher?"

He did not listen, he only swallowed the
pie, GLUP. Then he said,

"MORE, MORE I MUST HAVE MORE!
MORE MICE PIES OR I'LL EAT *YOU*!"

I said, "But Uncle!"

He said, "BUT WHAT!!" And he
HUFFED and he PUFFED and he PUFFED
and he HUFFED.

I thought Oh no, he will kill me dead.
But I got my braveness up. I said, "There are

lots more pies hidden in the forest! You can
have them *but*, teaching first, pies after."

And guess what, he went all nice! He
said, "OH MY DEAR SPLENDID HAN-
SUM NEPHEW, PLEASE LET ME
TEACH YOU BAGS OF BADNESS."

He says we start
lessons tomorrow.
And tonight I am
sleeping in the *dorm*!

Yours proudly,

Little

PS How do you like the posh notepaper?

Day 14

Dear Mum and Dad,

Slept in the dorm last night. It was nice but not as cosy and smelly as home, boo shame. I wished some other pupils were there. Never mind because guess what, I found a big mirror and had a pillow fight with myself!

I got up early and did grrrrs for the practice. I have got a bit of a sore throat now, but I think I am quite scary. Then I sharpened my pencils and colouring-in crayons and pointed them all the same way so I was ready for class.

My first lesson that I learnt today was this. Small wolves clean up, big wolves sit down and watch telly.

Bit sad, eh? I thought we would be doing
Badness, but no.
Uncle got huffy and
puffy and said all his
pupils must clean the
blackboard, flit the
flies, polish the desks,
shoo the spiders, and
scrub the floor, win-
dows and lavs.

So I did. It took me a long time, nearly
till dark. Uncle said, "GRRRR, WHY
ARE YOU SO SLOW, YOU SISSY?"

I said, "I am not slow but everything is
filthy dirty."

That was the wrong answer. Uncle sent
me to bed and ate my supper.

Yours hohummly,

Littly

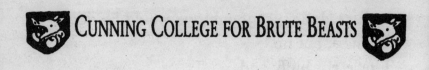

Day 15

Dear Mum and Dad,

No cleaning today, hooray! And guess what, I have learnt 2 Rules of Badness already!

I found a quite clean notebook in one of the desks and I wrote in it

Uncle came in the classroom. He was shining up his big gold BAD badge with his sleeve. I said, "Hum nice! When will I get my badge?"

Uncle was nasty, he said, "NOT UNTIL YOU KNOW THE 9 RULES OF BADNESS AND THAT WILL TAKE YOU YEARS AND YEARS BECAUSE YOU ARE NOT CRAFTY ENOUGH TO FIND THEM OUT SWIFTLY."

I said, "Maybe not, but I am still going to try my hardest."

Uncle said, "VERY WELL, MY CLUE-LESS CUB, LET US START WITH A STORY WHICH MIGHT HELP YOU OUT. 2 RULES OF BADNESS ARE HIDDEN IN IT, BUT YOU ARE MUCH TOO SMALL AND HOPELESS TO FIND THEM!"

I said, "Never mind, tell me the story anyway."

So Uncle smiled his big horrible smile and he began.

"ONCE UPON A TIME THERE WERE 3 LITTLE PIGGIES AND THEY GOT ON MY NERVES SINGING

THAT THEY WERE NOT AFRAID OF
BIGBAD WOLF. AND THEY KEPT
GOING HA-HA-HA-HA-HA ALL THE
TIME. SO I HUFFED AND I HUFFED
AND I PUFFED THEIR HOUSES
DOWN AND ATE THEM."

I made a joke. I said,
"Gosh, Uncle, fancy
eating their houses!
Were the bricks tasty?"

Uncle said, "SILENCE, SPECK! THAT
IS NOT FUNNY! GGRRRR, I ONCE
HAD A BLARSTED DREADFUL
ACCIDENT WITH A BRICK HOUSE.
I NEARLY BLEW MY HEAD OFF
TRYING TO HUFF IT DOWN. SO
YOU BLINKING BLUNKING KEEP
QUIET ABOUT BRICK HOUSES!"

I said, "Well now I think I can make a
guess. I know what Rules 1 and 2 are,
Uncle! The answer is:

RULE 1. HUFF AND PUFF A LOT.
RULE 2. SAY LOADS OF RUDE WORDS."

Uncle got very angry. He said,
"GGGRRR! HOW DO YOU KNOW
THAT? YOU MUST HAVE CHEATED!
SOMEBODY TOLD YOU THOSE
RULES!"

I said, "Nobody told me! I guessed!" And
I wrote Rule 1 and 2 in my Book of Badness.

He went, "GGGRR!" and bit a lump out
of the sink.

Love from

Littly

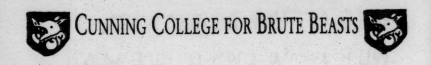

Day 16

Dear Mum and Dad,

My 3rd day at Cunning College, and Uncle has stopped my lessons. He said there was nothing in the larder and I must go for food. I said, "Do you mean go to the shops? They are miles away."

He said, "SILENCE, MOANER! I HAVE NO MONEY, THEREFORE YOU WILL HAVE TO HUNT FOR OUR LUNCH IN FRETTNIN FOREST. BRING ME BACK A SQUIRREL BURGER, SWIFTLY, SWIFTLY."

I thought, funny, didn't that fox say he had bags of money hidden somewhere?

Oh dear, I spent ages trying to catch squirrels but I am hopeless at climbing trees. All I got was just some peabugs and earwigs for crunchy snacks.

Uncle went mad for a bit when I got back. He growled and kicked the stuffing out of the sofa. (He was quite scary but no more than Dad.) Then he ate the crunchy snacks and went to bed. He says it is new moon tomorrow, therefore he must get his strength up.

He would not even stop to tick my work in my Book of Badness, so not much Badgework yet. But do not fret and frown, I will soon be the baddest boy in the pack.

Yours youbettly,

L

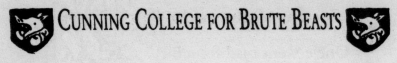

Day 17

Dear M and D,

Boring boring boring. The most interesting thing today was it rained. Here is a poem I wrote called BORING SNORING.

It's raining it's boring
Uncle Bigbad is snoring
He howls all night
And he looks such a sight
And he never gets up when you call him.

This is a pic of me trying to wake him up.

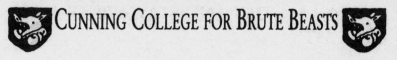

New moon
Day 18

Dear Mum and Dad,

I feel like running away. It is rubbish here. No other pupils to play with, nothing to do, nothing to eat and you do not even get letters because of Uncle eating the postmen. I am starting to wonder if he is as brainy as he keeps saying he is. I have not learnt a thing except huffing and puffing and no new rude words either. I could stand it if Yeller was here to talk to, or even Smellybreff. I am a very lone wolf.

I have not seen much of Uncle since I took him his breakfast in bed. I said to him, "Here is your nice breakfast, now can you teach me the 3rd Rule of Badness?"

He said, "DO NOT DISTURB, I MUST

SLEEP ALL DAY AND STAY AWAKE ALL NIGHT."

I said, "Doing what?"

He said, "BEING A TERROR!" And then he said, "FLY AND FLEE, SMALL FLUFFBALL. GO OUTSIDE AND DO SOME QUIET HUFFING PRACTICE."

I did what he said, I huffed and puffed in the garden but it made me giddy just blowing dandylions.

Yours fedduply,

Little

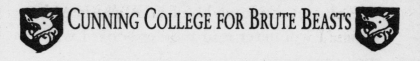

Day 19

Dear Mum and Dad,

It is gone midnight and I cannot sleep. Uncle is on the roof, howling and howling at the new moon. He goes on and on. He is not being a terror, just a pain.

I cannot stand it.

Please let me come home and I promise *promise* I will never read another book, I will stick crayons up my nose more often, I will be rotten to Smellybreff and hide his spoon and pusher all the time, I will be a real ~~noosunce~~ ~~newsens~~ pain. Only don't make me stay in this blunking blarsted silly college. (See, I can say lots of rude words now. Can't you just be proud of that?) I cannot bear another night of Uncle's howling.

Yours ~~despritly,~~ desperately,

Littly

Day 20

Dear Mum and Dad,

Guess what, we had a visitor today, thrill thrill. It was a tall man with a berry on his head and a whistle on a string. I thought yippee, somebody to try my ggrrrs on. I opened the door (eeeeee-arrrrrr) and did my best ggrrrr.

He patted me on the head and said, "So sorry to bother you, sonny jim, but we are camping nearby. Could you possibly do something to mend the burglar alarm that kept going off last night on your roof. My poor cubs never slept a wink. Good morning."

I said, "Fly and flee immediate-lee!" But he did not seem to notice, he just saluted and said, "Thank you very much, sonny jim, have a nice day."

He did not fool me with that story about cubs. No way he is a wolf. I wonder what trick he is up to.

I cannot ask Uncle, he is asleep again. Ah, well, must go and look for something to pounce on, I am starving.

Yours peckishly,

Littly

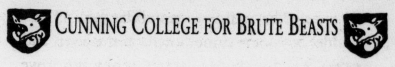

Day 20
Night-time

Dear Mum and Dad,

Guess what, just when I thought, Oh no, I will never learn any more Rules of Badness, I found out Number 3!

This is what happened 1st thing today. Uncle was up on the roof. I was having a good sniff round the kitchen looking for a snack. And do you know what? I found *loads* of food. There was ratflakes, some dried vole, even half a moosecake! They were hidden in the back of a cupboard, and Uncle said there was no food in the house! The fox was right, he *is* a miser!

It made me stop and wonder. Perhaps Uncle has got some hidden treasure somewhere, after all!

I did not have time to search because all of a suddenly, Uncle came down off the roof. Such a bad mood! He told me it was a waste of time howling because the moon cheats. He said, "IT COMES NEARER AND NEARER BUT JUST WHEN YOU HAVE HOWLED YOUR HEAD OFF AND YOU THINK IT IS CLOSE ENOUGH FOR YOU TO TAKE A NICE BIG CHEESY BITE OUT OF IT, IT BACKS AWAY!"

Then he crawled into bed all grumbly.

Thus and therefore Uncle was fibbing! He was not trying to be a terror, just trying to get a free snack! What a greedy guts!

So guess what, I do not think Uncle always tells the truth. And that is how I found out Rule 3. I wrote it down in my Book of Badness.

RULE 3. FIB YOUR HEAD OFF.

Yours sherlockholmesly,

ME

Day 21

Dear Mum and Dad,

Bit tired today. I could not sleep because of thinking about the man with the whistle. Do you remember, he came to complain about Uncle being a burglar alarm? I have not told Uncle about him yet because I have got an idea. I am going to play a trick on that man, and then Uncle will most likely think, AHA! THAT IS A BLUNKING BLARSTED GOOD TRICK, SO NOW I MUST TEACH THAT CRAFTY NEPHEW OF MINE LOADS MORE BADNESS.

My best idea so far is, stuff something up the man's whistle. Crafty, eh? But I am still trying to think of something even badder than that. See? I am trying my hardest to be like Uncle, so you can be proud of me.

I looked all over the forest to find the camp where the man said he keeps his cubs, but no luck yet. Still, I found a cottage not far from here. A girl lives there. I watched her all morning to see if she would be fun to play with, but not really. She is too busy dressing up in red riding hoods and taking picnics to her granny, etc., boo shame. I am quite surprised Uncle has not eaten her yet. But maybe he has noticed that her dad is a woodcutter with large muscles and a big sharp axe.

My best news is, the girl took her dad a picnic and guess what, she dropped 2 chicken legs out of her basket, yum yum!

I am saving them (big secret).

Your crafty

Little Wolf

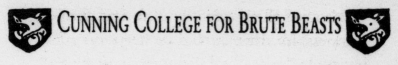

Day 22

Dear Mum and Dad,

I gave Uncle one of the chicken legs I found and that made him be in a really good mood. So I said to him, "I know where there are lots more."

Then I got my book out and I said, "Uncle, I have written down 3 rules in my Book of Badness. Can you teach me Number 4?"

He said, "PERHAPS, BUT HOW MANY MORE OF THESE DELICIOUS CHICKEN LEGS CAN I HAVE?"

I said, "One now, Uncle, lots more later." (Only one really but I was thinking of Rule 3, fib your head off.)

He said, "I ADORE CHICKEN LEGS SO I WILL TELL YOU 2 RULES!"

I copied them carefully in my book of Badness, like this:

RULE 4. IF IT SQUEAKS, EAT IT.
RULE 5. BLOW EVERYBODY ELSE.

This is easy cheesy!! Soon I will know all 9 Rules of Badness.

petit wolf (french)

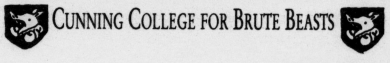 CUNNING COLLEGE FOR BRUTE BEASTS

Day 23

Dear Mum and Dad,

I keep on at Uncle to teach me more
Rules of Badness but he has got very
snappish. He just says HUFFING AND
PUFFING all the time and I know that one.
Also he has moved the food in the kitchen to
a new hiding place, I think he thinks I have
been nibbling (I ask you, would I? hem
hem).

Yore puzzled

Littly

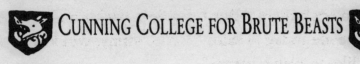

Day 24

Dear Mum and Dad,

Got another Rule, hooray! It is

RULE 6. DO YOUR DIRTIEST EVERY DAY.

Uncle has got a big mirror in his room, all nice and dusty. He spent 4 hours yesterday gazing at himself and he must have just scribbled it in the dust without noticing. (He loves himself *so* much!)

Quick as a chick I put it down in my Book of Badness. Then I decided to go exploring and see if I could find anybody to do my dirtiest on. I went through Frettnin Forest and right over Dark Hills, looking for the man with the whistle and his cubs. And guess what, I found their camp down by Lake Lemming!

Sad to say, I could not think of a good trick

to trick them. But I did do a trick on a beetle today. I said, "Hello, sonny, would you like to play a game?"

So he said, "OK, why not?" So I said, "Go on then, say, 'What is the time, Mister Wolf'."

So he said, "Why?" So I said, "You will see in a minute." So he said, "OK. What is the time, Mister Wolf?" and I said, "DINNER TIME, har, har!"

He was quite tasty.

Wait till Uncle hears that, he will make me a prefect, I bet!

Your best cub (tell that to Smellybreff, he will go mad, har har),

Little

Day 25, I think
(just my luck if it is wensdie
I can not spell it!)

Dear Mum and Dad,

I told Uncle about tricking that beetle yesterday. He did not make me a prefect, he got all jealous instead. He said, "GGGGRRRRUBBISH, THAT IS NOT WICKED, THAT IS A GOODY-GOODY TRICK!"

Being a bit upset, I went out for a wander in the forest and guess what, I bumped into the man with the whistle! He said, "Hello, sonny jim. I am the leader of a pack of cub scouts. We are camping down by Lake Lemming. Tomorrow we plan to have a barbecue. We hope you can join us. Here is an invitation." I snatched the invitation and said my scariest

CUB SCOUT
BARBECUE
7 o'clock
by LAKE
LEMMING

GGRRRAAH but he said, "Oh dear, have you got a sore throat, sonny jim? Have a cough sweet, must dash now."

I ran back and told Uncle. He said, "A CUB SCOUT BARBECUE? YUM YUM, I LOVE CUB SCOUTS, DELICIOUS."

I said, "Uncle, I think the pack leader wants us to go and eat his *sausages* not his cub scouts."

But Uncle would not listen. He said, "I KNOW THEIR MOTTO, IT IS BE PREPARED. THUS AND THEREFORE I SHALL PREPARE SOME FOR THE OVEN AND THE REST FOR THE POT. NONE FOR YOU THOUGH, GGGRRRR."

Boo shame, Uncle is too good at doing the dirty.

Yours upsettly,

Little

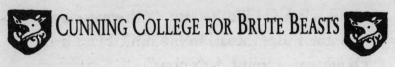

Day 26

Dear Mum and Dad,

Had an outdoor lesson today, learnt Rule 7 and Uncle bit me.

At 1st Uncle was in a good mood because he was plotting. He decided to catch the cub scouts by a trick called charming. (Have you heard of it? Nor had I.) Anyway, Uncle showed me how you do charming on a mole.

We went to this field all covered in mole hills. I said, "What are we doing here, Uncle?"

He said, "I AM SHOWING YOU CHARMING. SO SHUT UP, YOU SISSY FLUFFBALL, OBSERVE AND LEARN FROM THE MASTER."

I watched and took notes. First he lay flat on his tummy. Then he smiled a big horrible smile. Then he shouted down the mole hole, "GGGRRRR! LISTEN, MOLEY, COME OUT OR I WILL BASH YOUR HILLS IN!!!" And lastly, he took a running jump and skwish, he skwished the mole hill with his great big horrible feet. I made notes in my Book of Badness like this

How to do Charming:
    big smile,
    running jump,
    skwish hills

I added:

Say horrible growly things about bashing.

There were loads and loads of hills, Uncle took ages jumping on them. And do you know what? We never even saw the mole.

He was hiding underground.

I said to Uncle, "I think charming is rubbish." That is when he went mad and bot my bittom. (Other way round, sorry.)

He said, "WAIT TILL YOU SEE ME CHARMING THOSE CUB SCOUTS TOMORROW!"

Yours sorebottly,

Little

(nice pic of a mole, eh?)

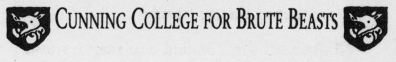

Day 27

Dear Mum and Dad,

What a muckupp! Uncle is in bed with a headache and he did not catch one cub scout to eat, not even a sausage. I will tell you about it.

Uncle sat and cooled his sore feet in a bath in front of the fire all morning. Suddenly he said, "AH, NOW I AM READY FOR SOME PROPER CHARM-ING." He drank his bathwater, burped and dried his feet on the curtains, then off we went to Windy Ridge. It was just before the sun hid.

It was frozz up on the ridge, it made your teeth ache. Uncle said we had to smile a big smile and stand in the North wind till it got stuck. It took *ages*. Then we had to ker-lump through the forest in the dark and take our smiles to Lakeside Meadow.

Talk about hard, finding it in the dark, and
we were glad of the warm campfire.
Uncle stood frozz in the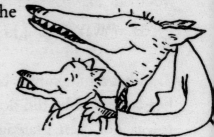
firelight looking
all horrible,
like he had his tail
caught in a gate.

The pack leader came up to us.
I thought, Oh no, trouble.

But he said, "Welcome, sir, welcome,
sonny jim, would you like something to eat?"

I was going to say I would have a nice hot
sausage but Uncle smiled his stuck-on smile
and said, "GGRRRR! YESSS! GIVE ME
YOUR CUB SCOUTS OR I'LL HUFF
AND I'LL PUFF AND I'LL *BLOW* YOUR
TENTS DOWN!"
The pack leader shouted, "Quick, boys,
emergency!" He blew his whistle and bing,
all the cub scouts jumped into their tents
and zipped up.

Uncle huffed and he puffed his hardest.
Nothing happened. The tents dented a bit
but they stayed standing up. Uncle's cheeks
went out like balloons and he got redder and
redder and redder. Then all of a suddenly, he
twizzled round six times and fell on his nose.

I have written down Rule 7 in my Book of
Badness. This is it.

RULE 7. DO CHARMING. SNEAKY SMILES.

I think Rule 7 is rubbish. I had to drag
Uncle all the way home by his tail.

Yours tiredoutly,

Little

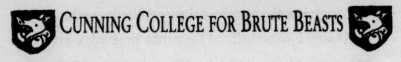

Day 28

Dear Mum and Dad,

Uncle has still got a bad head and tailache. He says he is dying (hem hem) and will not get out of bed. I gave him the bonnet I took from Mister Twister at Borderlands Market. I said, "Here, this will keep your head warm." He put it on, then he told me to depart swiftly, swiftly, so I went exploring in the forest.

I have been thinking about the tents that the cub scouts had. The strings and the pegs were in just right. You could never blow them down, even I could see that and I am just a learner. Are you quite sure you want me to be like Uncle? Sometimes I wonder what is so brilliant about him.

Anyway, soon I came to a new track. It leads to an empty place in the forest made by the woodcutter cutting down the trees there. And guess what, there was that girl with the red hood all by herself with a picnic basket. I thought, Oh good – more chicken, I am starving. But just then, her granny came along.

And guess what? All of a suddenly, a cunning trick jumped in my head! In my mind I saw Uncle wearing the bonnet I got from Mister Twister!

I went back to Cunning College running, running, and I said, "Listen Uncle, I know how you can catch a nice tasty little girl with a red hood. Why not dress up as her granny!"

Uncle said I am the stupidest pupil he has ever had. He said no way will I ever get my Bad badge now.

I am all upset.

Sniff sniff from

Little

Day 29

Dear Mum and Dad,

Uncle jumped out of bed his earliest yet. He said he had thought of a brilliant way to trap that little red-hood girlie, wear a bonnet and pretend to be her granny!

I said, "Uncle, I told you that, that was my idea!!"

He said, "SO WHAT?" He said if I was a really clever, cunning bad wolf, I would keep my good ideas to myself and not blab them around. He said, "SO WRITE THAT IN YOUR STUPID BOOK OF BADNESS!"

I must be a slow learner. Still I have written it down. This is it.

RULE 8. DO NOT BLAB YOUR GOOD IDEAS.

Ho hum from

3 guesses

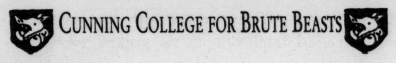

Day 30

Dear Mum and Dad,

Today I had to help Uncle get dressed up in his bonnet and granny dress and everything. He kept looking in the mirror going, "HUM, YESSS, VERY NICE, I THINK IT SUITS ME." So vain.

At last we got going to the grandma's house about tea time. Guess who went in and had all the fun. Yes, Uncle. He would not let me tie the old lady up or stick her in the wardrobe. He said my job was to stay outside and give a wolf-whistle if any wood-cutters came along.

I hid for a bit till Little Red Goodie-hoodie came along with a basket and tip-tapped at the door. You should have heard Uncle's granny-voice, it was rubbish!! Even Smellybreff can do better voices. I would have run a mile if I was that girl. But she is such a sad simple dimple, she walked right in.

It got so boring just doing nothing. I went off and chased a few snacks for my tea in the forest, but they jumped down their holes, boo, shame. Then I wandered off back to Cunning College.

Big roast supper for Uncle tonight, I 'spect.

But nothing for me.

Yours rumblytumly,

Littly

CUNNING COLLEGE FOR BRUTE BEASTS

Day 31

Dear M and D,

Dear oh dear, poor old Uncle. While I was off chasing snacks, the woodcutter came along and whacked him on the bonnet with the back of his axe. Also he split him in 2 and took Little Red Goodie-hoodie out of his tummy.

So guess what, Uncle is not feeling his best today. He said it is all my fault and so I must suffer too.

He made me sew him up and feed him rat soup every 2 hours. I am not allowed to listen to music. And no telly, no fun at all. He kept on and on at me about me being stupid stupid and said I could forget the BAD badge now, *no* chance.

I have been dashing about all over the

84

place finding vinegar and brown paper to wrap Uncle's head in. He will not let me fetch the doctor, he says it costs too much. Also he makes me sit by his bed and keep the flies off him, so boring.

I am a complete failure, so sorry.

Your hopeless cub,

Little

Dear Dum and Mad,

I do not know how to tell you. Something terrible has happened. I have been expelled from Cunning College.

Uncle is not fair. I nursed him and ran around for him. I even fanned him with a cabbage leaf to save using the electric fan. But all of a suddenly, he made me write a letter to Mister Twister at Borderlands Market, like this:

MY DEAR LONG LOST CHUM,

HOW FOOLISH I WAS TO FALL OUT WITH YOU AND SEND YOU AWAY, RUSH TO MY AID AND I WILL REWARD YOU HANSUMLY. I AM AT DEATH'S DOOR, ALL MY NEPHEW'S FAULT.

WHEN I AM BETTER, PERHAPS WE CAN MOVE NEAR A FARM AND WORRY

SHEEP TOGETHER.

HURRY. I AM ALL ALONE.
YOUR MELANCHOLY PARTNER,

BEEBEE WOLF

When I finished writing, Uncle said,
"GGGGRRRRR! NOW YOU CAN
BLINKING BLUNKING WELL BUZZ
OFF. I AM TOO POOR TO KEEP
YOU."

I said, "But, Uncle, I have only got 1
more Rule of Badness to learn! What about
my BAD badge?"

He said, "TOUGH LUCK. GET OUT.
YOU ARE MUCH TOO EXPENSIVE
FOR ME."

Then I made a big mistake. I said, "OO,
what a big miser! I bet you are rich really."

Uncle went crackers. He jumped out of
bed. He yelled, "THAT IS A FLIPPING
FLOPPING BIG WHOPPING LIE!!!

WHO TOLD YOU I HAVE GOT BAGS
OF GOLD STUFFED UP THE ...?"

He did not finish saying stuffed up the
where. He just threw cups and saucers at me
and screamed, "GET OUT!!!"

Now I am all by my ownly in Frettnin
Forest.

Your chuckoutly,

L Wolf

Dear Mum and Dad,

Just a short note to say goodbye and sorry. I have let the family down, specially Dad. I am a disgrace to the pack.

Do not worry, I am not coming home badgeless. I am going to hide myself deep in Frettnin Forest and hope that one day my yellow eyes will make friends with the dark and dampness.

Forgive and forget me. I shall change my name and stay far away.

Yours,

Shadow (my secret name)

Dear M and D,

Ahem. Me again. Just when I thought I was stuck being Shadow for ever! Uncle has given me 1 last chance, which is …

He says he might award me my BAD badge. But only if I pass his BIG SURVIVAL TEST.

(A) I must stay alive in Frettnin Forest with no shelter, no provisions, no nothing and

(B) I must bring him back something big and lipsmackerous to eat from the forest.

I have got exactly 1 week to pass this test. Which is a bit too hard for me, I think, but I shall have a go.

Yours once morely,
Littly

PS Did I ever tell you camping out is my worst thing? Well, I think this might be even ~~worster~~ ~~worser~~ ~~worstest~~ ~~incomfortabler~~ more nasty.

Dear Mum and Dad,

Just a postcard before I curl up, no post box near. Still it is something to do.

Brrr, frozz here in the open, worse than the tent even. I looked all day for a cave but they have all got huge big grizzly bears in. Also v. little to eat.

Oh yes, that reminds me, I hurt myself trying a new snack today. What do they call them, hedgehogs, is it? Talk about hot, it really burnt my mouth. How was I to know you are supposed to peel them first?

Anyway, no way was that snack lipsmacker-ous. Dear oh flip, I do not think I will *ever* pass Uncle's BIG TEST.

Bbbrrr.

Your chilly boy,

Little

Dear M and D,

As you can see from the above address, I have moved. Not that it is any more comfy, I am wedged in like a tight nut in a shell. Dear oh dear, what a rubbish shelter, and only a few grubs to chew.

At least the rain has stopped. About time because my fur has gone soggy like a rat in a gutter. It makes you feel all spooky when it stops pattering on the leaves.

I thought I heard something rustle in the bushes outside just now. Maybe it is Uncle come to check me out. But he would not bother, so who is it????

Yours Oo-erly,

Littly

Dear Mum and Dad,

Oh no, trapped!!!
Now who is the sad sim-
ple dimple? Me! The
whistly pack leader will
put me in a zoo tomor-
row, I know it. And I
cannot even stand my
bedroom, let alone cages!!

You know I said about rustling? Well, it
was 2 cub scouts crawling through the
bushes. I thought, Funny, what are they
doing in the forest? Then I thought, Yum
yum, I am starving and scouts look more
lipsmackerous than hedgehogs any day. I will
pounce on them silently, eat 1 and save the
other for Uncle. Then I will pass the BIG
TEST, yippee.

Sad to say, my cunning plan went a bit wrong. P'raps it was my rumbling tum, I do not know, but all of a suddenly, 1 cub scout turned round and saw me lurking. He said, "I say, old chap, you do not look quite well. Can we assist you in some way?"

All of a suddenly, everything went black and when I woke up in their camp, oh no! I was zipped up to my chin in a padded bag and laid down inside a tent! Then the whistly pack leader came along saying, "Oh dear, sonny jim, you are skinny as a rake, we had better fatten you up."

Do they have fat wolf cubs in zoos? Oo-er, maybe they are fattening me up for the cooking pot!!! Please do not tell Smells or Yeller if I end up as stew.

Yours capturedly,

Little

Dear Mum and Dad,

(Arrrooooo!)

Burn my last letter,
I am *sooo* lucky!

I am not on the menu, I am a guest
(somebody you have to stay). That zippy bag
was not a trap, it was for sleeping, hmmm
cosy! They put me in it for *first aid*!

And listen to this bit, the pack leader says
they are going to return me to the wild as
soon as I am ready!! BUT *not before I have
had loads and loads of grub to build up my
strength*!

I have just had stew, potatoes and bakebeans. Brilliant, specially the bakebeans, I
love them, kiss kiss!

The boys who found me in the forest are called Dave and Sanjay. They were out playing the Wide Game which is trying to creep back to the camp by the lake without your friends seeing you. Today they are going to teach it to me and also something called Campcraft, which is great because true I am quite crafty, but my camping is rubbish. I aim to get good and surprise Uncle.

Nip Smellybreff for me and tell him not long now before he sees his ~~hansum~~ handsome brother (this is me, he is the ugly one going boo-hoo!!!).

Yours,

Tubby tum (get it?)

Dear Mum and Dad,

Today we did putting up a shelter; how to stay alive if you get lost; making a shoe-rack out of sticks and string; lighting a fire and nkots (is that right?). Now I know just the right nkot for tying up grandmothers and baby brothers, so watch out, Smells! Tomorrow the pack leader says he will show us mapping and compass-work and tracking. Handy for a wolf, eh? A lot better than Uncle Bigbad's lessons, if you ask me (do not tell him). Anyway, I can pass Uncle's BIG TEST easy cheesy now, I bet.

And guess what, if you join the Cub Scouts properly you can get *loads* of badges!! But there is 1 problem, Dave says you have to make a Cub Scout promise. So tough on me

99

because how can you be BAD *and* make a promise? It is too goody-goody.

Probably I shall stay here 1 more day and then go back to the forest. This is my plan: set up a brilliant camp and wait for Uncle to come and be impressed. My only small problem is finding something big and lips-mackerous to eat, but maybe something will turn up.

Then I can pass my BIG TEST, finish properly at Cunning College, get my BAD badge and you can all be proud of me. Tell Yeller to get ready because we are going to have a wicked time when I get home! And he will say, "Hello, Little Wolf, cor, you are just like your Uncle, only badder."

Arrroooo!

~~kisses~~ ~~tonks~~
~~loake~~

Littly

PS Sanjay says there is a k in nots which sounds daft but I have written one in case.

Dear Mum and Dad,

Lots to tell you. It's a good thing I like writing. Guess what, the Pack Leader is an Akela, same as Dad!!

Cub Scouts are great! Did you know you can do *loads* of badges if you join. Akela said if I stayed, I could study for Camper, Explorer, Navigator, Book Reader, etc. They even have one called Animal Lover. I said, Oh arrroooo, I am an Animal Lover, I love rabbit rolls. But Akela said, Animal Lover is not an eating badge. Ah well. Pity.

I am really good at putting up tents now and the Wide Game and telling stories round the campfire. Today I told all about Uncle and Cunning College and the 9 Rules of Badness, and how important it is for me to get my BAD badge.

Everybody asked me what are the 9 Rules

of Badness. I said, "Sorry, I only know 8, will they do?" and they said, "Yes, tell us." So I said,

"1. Huff and puff a lot.
2. Say loads of rude words.
3. Fib your head off.
4. Blow everyone else.
5. If it squeaks, eat it.
6. Do your dirtiest every day.
7. Do charming.
8. Do not blab your good ideas."

Dave said, "That is interesting because the Cub Scout rules are just the opposite, and they are:

1. Do your best.
2. Think of others.
3. Do good turns."

I said, "Har har, good joke, Dave!" Then Akela said, "So, sonny jim, was it that big bad fellow who tried to blow our tents down taught you all those nasty rules?"

So I said, "Yes, it was Uncle Bigbad."

So Akela said, "Well, I am sorry, sonny jim, but I think your uncle should not be a teacher. He should be locked away. He is a cruel, savage brute."

I said, "Gosh, thanks a lot, Akela. Uncle would be so happy to hear you say those kind words!"

Yours newsily,

L

Dear Mum and Dad,

Today is my best day so far since I started having adventures. Guess what, I have made HISTORY!

This is what happened. I was feeling a bit sad and sorry because today was my last day with the cub scouts. I was in my tent packing my rucksack in the cub scout way (without pointy things sticking in your back). Then Sanjay came and said I was wanted.

The cub scouts all made a ring and I stood in the middle. Then Akela said, "Just before you go, sonny jim, we want you to take 1 or 2 things to remember us by." He said, "You have made the last few days very special for Lakeside Camp. Because you are the first real wolf cub we have met. We are proud to be part of your Great Adventure, and thus and therefore, we would like to make a

presentation. So here is your special CUB
SCOUT ADVENTURE AWARD with
certificate and badge."

Can you *beleeeeve* it, a BADGE! At last!!!
Plus they gave me a load of provisions
including chocklit fingers, potty noodles and
3 WHACKING big tins of bakebeans
(canteen size), because they are my favourite.

Arrrooooooooo

from The Adventurer

Dear Mum and Dad,

I am deep in the forest where it is so dark
and dismal you would not beleeeeeve! Even
the bats wear glasses (only kidding). But I
am not scared 1 bit!

Have made this *excellent* shelter out
of sticks and leaves (a bivouac if
you want to know the proper cub
scout word, hem hem). Also I
have got a fire going with 1
match (stones all round to
keep it from spreading, v.
important).

I am *so* warm and cosy, it is brilliant!
And guess what I have cooked? Alphabetti
spaghetti, it comes in tins. I will bring
you some and show you how to open
them. There you are, I have done a

SMELLYBREFF in spaghetti and stuck it on the page for him. Good, eh?

    I am just waiting till midnight so that I can creep back to Cunning College and surprise Uncle. Because I have passed my BIG TEST. I am still alive after 1 week and I have got some lipsmackerous stuff for him to eat.

    So DYB DYB DOB DOB to you!

      Yours campcraftily,

        Little

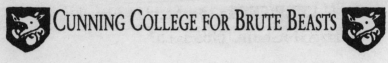

Dear Mum and Dad,

Big shock!! Arrived
back at Cunning College
and found Uncle all tied
up with rope and skinnier
than ever! Cunning College
was a mess, desks tipped
over, furniture upset, rubbish
all over. He said, "GGRRR!
UNTIE ME, SWIFTLY,
SWIFTLY, WHERE HAVE
YOU BEEN?" I said,
"Having an adventure.
Where is Mister Twister?"

He said, "HE ATTACKED ME! HE
TIED ME UP! HE WAS TRYING TO
FIND MY MONEYBAGS AND NOW HE

HAS WRECKED MY SCHOOL. THE
BLINKING BLUNKER!"

I said, "What moneybags, Uncle? I
thought you were poor."

He said, "GGGRRR! SILENCE,
SQUIRT! CLEAN UP THIS PLACE AND
GET ME SOMETHING TO EAT! I
MUST LIE DOWN ON THE COUCH."

I said, "OK, I will tidy up and I will give
you something lipsmackerous to eat. So now
I have passed the BIG TEST will you give
me a BAD badge after?"

Uncle said, "WHAT A MAGNIFICENT
LITTLE PUPIL YOU ARE. OF COURSE
YOU SHALL HAVE A BAD BADGE!
BUT FOOD FIRST, BADGE AFTER-
WARDS."

So exciting! Must stop now because lots
of work to be done.

Yours with a big Arrrooooo!

Little

CUNNING COLLEGE FOR BRUTE BEASTS

Day 44

Dear Mum and Dad,

What a big cheater Uncle is! Now I am all down and dumpy again!

I cleaned up the whole college, picked up, swept up, scrubbed up, mopped up and put away, phew. Then Uncle just gobbled up all my chocklit fingers and he wolfed down my potty noodles. He is such a greedy guts he did not bother to cook them or take them out of their plastic potties. Then he had a long long zizz on the couch.

When he woke up this morning he said he was starving hungry again. He bashed me with the board rubber and made me cook him breakfast. I said, "But I have passed my test! I lived in the forest by myself and I stayed alive. Plus I gave you something big and lipsmackerous for tea yesterday. So give me my BAD badge and let me go!"

He said, "OH, CERTAINLY CERTAINLY, CROSS MY HEART, STRAIGHT AFTER BREAKFAST, YOU CAN TRUST *ME*!"

I am down and dumpy because now I will have to cook him some of my special bake-beans and I was saving them, 1 for me, 1 for you and Smells, and 1 for Yeller.

More later on. 3 boos for Uncle.

Little

Boo
Boo Boo

Day 44 part 2
(after breakfast)

Dear Mum and Dad,

This is a bit sad but no presents for any-body. Sorry.

After I lit the fire, I put on the great big pot and filled it right up to the brim with my canteen-size tin of bakebeans. When the beans were nice and hot, Uncle went extra dribbly and he said, "GET A BIG BIG SPOON! FEED ME FEED ME, SWIFTLY, SWIFTLY!"

I said, "Careful, Uncle, bakebeans are gorgeous but don't eat too fast. Look at what the label says. Beware of the jumping beanbangs!"

But he would not look, he would not listen. He got huffy and puffy and he threw the spoon in the corner. He yelled, "TOO SMALL! GET THE LADLE AND FEED ME FEED ME, SWIFTLY, SWIFTLY!" So I did. He swallowed the lot in 35 secs. Then he licked his lips and his voice went all weak and he said, "What about 1 more tin?"

So number 2 tin that I was saving for Yeller went into the pot, canteen-size again. When the bakebeans were hotted up, I fed them to Uncle with the ladle. Talk about a quick eater, it was like stoking the boiler. Uncle said (weak voice), "Just 1 more tiny tin?"

I said, "But they are my treat for my mum and dad and Smellybreff, I am saving them. I want to take them home with my BAD badge so they can be proud of me. Besides, remember the label. Beware of the jumping beanbangs!"

But he said, "GGGGGRRR, WHO CARES ABOUT BLUNKING BLARSTED BEANBANGS! GET THE COAL SHOVEL AND FEED ME, SWIFTLY, SWIFTLY!!!"

So number 3 tin that I was saving for you and Smells went into the pot, the biggest tin of bakebeans you can get.

Uncle opened his mouth wide as wide and I shovelled in all the bakebeans with the coal shovel, swiftly, swiftly.

Then he smacked his horrible lips and he rolled his horrible eyes and he said, "NOT ENOUGH, I MUST HAVE MORE! DASH BACK TO LAKESIDE CAMP AND GET LASHINGS MORE BAKEBEANS, SWIFTLY, SWIFTLY!"

I said, "But Uncle, my BAD badge, you promised!"

He said, "HAR HAR YOU SAD SUCKER! IT IS TIME I TOLD YOU RULE NUMBER 9. AND RULE NUMBER 9 IS ...

NEVER TRUST A BIG BAD WOLF!"

I wish I had thought of that before.

Yours badgelessly,

Littly

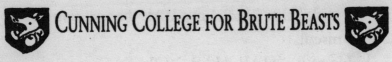

Dear Mother and Father,

Um what can I say, Uncle had a slight accident last night.

So I shall be quite busy burying him etc.

Please excuse short note.

Love

Little

Dear Mum and Dad,

Gosh what a tiring day yesterday. Soon after the accident, Akela and the cub scouts came. They helped me look for Uncle. We searched all morning but the only thing we found was his whiskers and his bonnet. So it did not take long digging a grave, very small. But it took ages carving a nice message on his gravestone, Akela said it is quite good rhyming and true, what do you think.

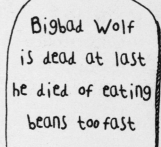

Bigbad Wolf is dead at last he died of eating beans too fast

This afternoon, found his gold BAD badge, it was hanging from the rafters.

More tomorrow.

Yours wornly,

Little

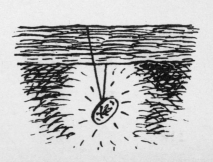

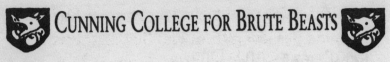

Day 47

Dear Mum and Dad,

I forgot to tell you how Uncle died. Sorry, I was a bit busy.

It was a suddenly thing. Because after Uncle scoffed all the bakebeans, suddenly there was this great big loud noise in the night, it made me jump. I thought Oh blow, Uncle is riding his motorbike round the furniture. But no, it was not a motorbike, it was just him jumping round holding his tummy, going POP-POP-POP-KERBANG! POP-POP-POP KERBANG!!!

I said, "Oh no, Uncle, you have got the jumping beanbangs from scoffing all those beans with the shovel! Best to stay in bed and open the window. But please, Uncle, whatever you do, do not go near the fire."

But he would not listen, he went mad. He said, "GET ME A LOG TO LUMP YOUR HEAD WITH!" And his great big eyes were rolling and his great big teeth were shining and his great big kerbangs were kerbanging.

I said, "Please keep away from the fire, Uncle!"

He said, "YOU CAN'T TRICK ME WITH YOUR PLEASES AND YOUR GOODY-GOODY WAYS." And he chased me round and round. Then he said his last words. He said,

"I'LL BOOM, I'LL BANG, I'LL BASH YOU FOR THIS!!! YOU BOOM YOU BANG YOU *BAD* LITTLE WOLF!!!"

Those were his last words because then he bent down by the fire to pick up a log to lump me with and

He exploded. Shame, eh? (In a way.) That is when the chimney fell over. It is lying in the garden now.

Yours sorry about not mentioning beforely,

L

Dear Mr and Mrs Moneybags and
 Baby Posh, ᴬ

Aha, tricked you! You thought this letter
was for somebody else I bet! But no, you
ARE posh and moneybags now. Because ,
guess what, Uncle was telling big fat fibs
about being poor!! (Rule 3.)

I was in the garden just now, feeling like
mucking about for a bit. The chimney was
lying among the flowers. So I thought, I
know, I will just have a quick game of
chimney sweeps, I like getting sooty. And in
I crawled. It was very funny and squeezy.
But the soot was *so* tickly, it made my nose
tickle. So I went Ah-hah-hah-TishINKLE!

And do you know what the TishINKLE

was? It was GOLD!!! BAGS AND BAGS
OF IT!!! So THAT is where Uncle had
stuffed it. Up the chimney!!!

Now we are *RICH*.

I have drawn me with Uncle's gold and his
big gold BAD badge on my chest. I have
awarded it to myself.

Yours deservingly,

L B Wolf (B for BAD, get it?)

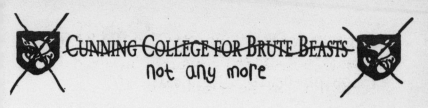
Midwood
Beastshire
BS1 4WW

Day 49

Dear Mum and Dad,

Do not worry, I shall be home soon. I am nearly ready but not quite.

I 'spect you will say Boohoo what is up? What is keeping our boy? He is rich, we are proud of him, he knows the 9 Rules of Badness, he has got a gold BAD badge. Plus he hates being away from home, it is his worst thing. So whyo whyo Y does he not zoom back to his nice smelly old lair?

Answer – ADVENTURES, I love them yum yum kiss kiss!! They are my best thing now. I want loads more. BUT (big

123

but) I do not like

1. going round and round in circles getting lost.
2. rain, ants etc down my neck.
3. falling-down tents.
4. problems chasing snacks, etc.
5. big fibbers tricking me and being nasty to me.

So I am joining the cub scouts properly. Yes, I have decided to do the promise and everything. Akela is going to bring Dave and Sanjay and the rest of the cub scouts to camp on the college lawn. Tomorrow they are going to help me study for my Navigator badge and my Explorer badge.

Then I shall be able to find my way home, and no mistakes!

See you soonly,

LBW

ADVENTURE ACADEMY

Day 50

Dear Mum and Dad,

I have changed my mind, I am not coming back to the Lair.

BUT do not howl sadly, because I am having such a good time doing my Navigator and Explorer badges. Plus now I have decided something. I do not wish to be like Uncle Bigbad. He was really Uncle Bigsad (get it?) because he had no friends. He was all huff and puff and hot air, so not surprising he went off bang, eh?

When I grow up I want to be ME, not just some big old horrible wolf that nobody trusts.

So guess what, I have decided to use some of the bags of money to start a new college in Frettnin Forest. And it will be called

Smellybreff and Yeller must come straight away. They can be teachers with me and it will be the best fun school in the world. Ever!!

Also I have made the cellar nice and smelly. That means you can come and be happy hibernaters ever after!! So

Arrrooooooooo

From

Little Bad Wolf

PS I am sending you 1 bag of money for fares etc. Buy smells some fake blood, some itchy powder, a whoopy cushion and get a pretend arrow through the head for Yeller. From now on, the tricks are on me!!!!!

DA DAA

Little Wolf's

Diary of Daring Deeds

Ian Whybrow
Illustrated by Tony Ross

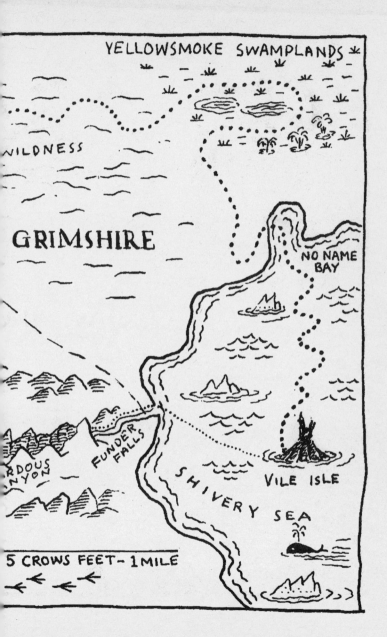

YELLOWSMOKE SWAMPLANDS

WILDNESS

GRIMSHIRE

NO NAME BAY

RDOUS NYON

FUNDER FALLS

SHIVERY SEA

VILE ISLE

5 CROWS FEET - 1 MILE

ADVENTURE ACADEMY

~~CUNNING COLLEGE FOR BRUTE BEASTS,~~

FOR DARING DEEDERS
FRETTNIN FOREST, BEASTSHIRE
HEADS: ~~BIGBAD WOLF, ESQ~~
LITTLE WOLF AND YELLER WOLF, ESQS

↑ Better, eh?

Dear Mum and Dad,

Please please PLEEEZ come and move in here, you said you would. Because my cuz Yeller is coming soonly to be a Head with me. Then we can get some pupils and start up Adventure Academy at last!!

I cannot wait hardly. I have found bags and bags of gold that Uncle Bigbad hid. That means I am RICH!! So we are going to have the best fun school ever. Also we are going to buy the best adventures in the world and put them in our playground. Then we can do daring deeds all the time, arrrooo!

5

Go on, I want you to come so you can be proud of me. Dad can retire from his work at Fang and Mauler and put his paws up. I have made the cellar all nice and smelly for you just like the Lair, so you can be happy hibernators for ever after.

Tell Smellybreff, yes, he can be a teacher because he is my baby bruv, but remember, me and Yeller are pack leaders, so no moaning.

Yours hurryuply,
Little

PS I am sending you some more gold so you can come by helicopter.

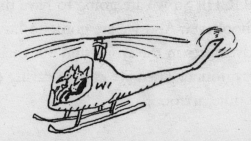

Dear Mum and Dad,

Posh paper, eh?

Big gales in the night. Tell the helicopter pilot I am a bit wurrid about him not seeing which part of the forest to come down in. So I have done HELLO HELLY LAND ON YOUR BELLY on a big mat for him.

Still no Yeller, boo shame, where is he? I wish he would hurry up because his ideas are just the best. Also I need him to help me with adverts for our school. I did one today but it is rubbish, look:

Adventure Acad
is good
So be a pupil,
not a pud

Well it is quite good rhyming. But shame I forgot to say about having fun and getting Daring Deed badges.

I 'spect Yeller is coming by slowcoach (get it?).

From your
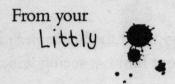
Littly

Dear Mum and Dad,

Arrrroooo! The postman came today with a big parcel saying, "Phew, heavy, hint hint." So I said to put it down in the hall and filled up his hands with gold.

He said, "Cor thanks, Master L, you are a lot nicer than your Uncle Bigbad. When he was here being Head of Cunning College for Brute Beasts, he used to eat postmen. He was a big horrible miser, he was. They say he had bags and bags of gold buried all over the place, but he never spent one penny, not like you. Good thing he went off bang if you ask me."

9

I gave him a small wolfly nip and a grrr for cheek and off he went happy and rich.

All of a suddenly the parcel went crickle crackle rip. Then out jumped a something saying a huge big RRRRRRRRAAAAAAAAAAAHHHH! and making my heart hop like frogs. And what was it? It was Yeller! I was so pleased to see his funny pointy face and my trick arrow through his head. And so good to hear his voice again, yelling, "HELLO LICKLE, HOW DID YOU LIKE MY TRICK PARCEL?"

Who else would think of a clever trick joke like posting yourself? Plus he brought me a posh present, a book for writing our adventures in. I am calling it *My Diary of Daring Deeds*, so 1 day all our grandcubs will read it and go, "Oo look, so brave," ect.

Yours proudly,
Little

ADVENTURE ACADEMY

FRETTNIN FOREST, BEASTSHIRE
HEADS; LITTLE WOLF AND YELLER WOLF, ESQS

Dear Mum and Dad,

Your crool letter you sent yesterday says you
will not move in here now. Whyo Y have you
changed your minds? Is it because Uncle
Bigbad went off bang and Dad blames me?
I bet it is. But I *told* him not to scoff all my
bakebeans with a shovel. He just did not listen,
being such a greedyguts.

PLEEEZ change your minds back again.

Yours upsettly,
Little

ADVENTURE ACADEMY

FRETTNIN FOREST, BEASTSHIRE
HEADS; LITTLE WOLF AND YELLER WOLF, ESQS

Dear Mum and Dad,

Murkshire is nice, yes, and the Lair is cosy, yes. But you will soon like Beastshire when you see it. Also Frettnin Forest is just the scaryest, Dad will love it.

But you say you think my plans are 2 showoff and cubbish. Dad says he does not agree with Adventure Playgrounds. He is so oldfashy. Because when you are rich and modern, you can buy adventures and be Daring Deeders at home. No need to go a long way for them. Or get killed, ect. See?

Yours pantingly,
Littly

ADVENTURE ACADEMY

FRETTNIN FOREST, BEASTSHIRE
HEADS; LITTLE WOLF AND YELLER WOLF, ESQS

Dear M and D,

Just to show you what you are missing. Look at this advert. Yeller found it in *Wolf Weekly* yesterday.

MISTER MARVO'S INSTANT ADVENTURES
SCARY BUT SAFE
ALSO WINTERPROOF AND UNBREAKABLE BY BRUTE BEASTS
DEMONSTRATIONS BY APPOINTMENT

See? It is brilliant. I am writing for a Mister Marvo appointment today! So go on, Mum and Dad, get on the helicopter quick!

Yours reallywantingly,
Littley

13

ADVENTURE ACADEMY

FRETTNIN FOREST, BEASTSHIRE
HEADS; LITTLE WOLF AND YELLER WOLF, ESQS

Dear Mum and Dad,

Yes I was surprised when the helicopter landed and baby bruv Smellybreff got out but not you. Yes I got your note off him, no he did not do a sick down his new sailor suit.

Yes I made sure he did not leave his ted in the helicopter. Yes I do know teddy is his best friend.

Yes I do understand that you are trusting me with your small darling baby pet till Springtime comes. Yes I know you will go RAVING MAD if I let anything bad happen to him.

Yes I promise I will keep writing and say if Smellybreff gets homesick or bangs his tiny nose, ect.

Yes you are right, it is furfluffingly chilly here and all the chestnuts have fallen.

I hope you enjoy your long winter zizz without us. When are you starting xactly? Also, are you sure you do not want to have your tiny Smells tucked up cosy in your bed?

Yours ??ly,
Little

ADVENTURE ACADEMY

FRETTNIN FOREST, BEASTSHIRE
HEADS; LITTLE WOLF AND YELLER WOLF, ESQS

Dear Mum and Dad,

Smells has been here 2 days now. He has been stupid and whiny and keeps messing my things up. Also, he will not call me and Yeller sir, even if we are Heads.

He is hopeless at Schools and playing teachers. But 1 thing he likes a lot is gold. I bought him a metal detector yesterday and off he went hunting for more of Uncle Bigbad's gold. He found 4 more bags. Now he wants a safe with a big key, PLUS combination lock.

Yours a bit fedupply,

Little

Dear Mum and Dad,

Guess what! A letter came from Mr Marvo today. He is coming soonly to tell us all about Instant Adventures for our playground, arrroooo! Yeller has got some brilliant BIG IDEAS for what we want, gokarts, motorbikes, roller-coasters, zipwire, dodgems, wall-of-death, helter skelter, parachute-jumper, arcade racing machines, ect! What is rubbish about that, Dad? Answer, nothing.

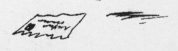

No winter zizzes for us cubs, we are much 2 excited.

Yours can'twaitly,

L

17

Dear Mum and Dad,

Smells wants me to send you a pic of his new safe so here it is.

Also he says har har he knows the number to open it but not me. So cubbish.

Your big boy,

L

18

Dear Mum and Dad,

Smells is OK today but a bit goldfeverish. He howled his head off till I gave him all my gold to put in his safe. Plus all the new bags he keeps finding with his metal detector.

This is what he does all the time. 1st he piles up gold in sixes (he only knows up to 6). Then he kisses each pile and puts them in his safe. Then he locks up. Then he whispers through the keyhole, "Night night darlings, sleepy tight. Daddy soon find you some more nice shiny friends to chink with."

What do you think about this?

Askingly
Little Wolf

19

ADVENTURE ACADEMY

FRETTNIN FOREST, BEASTSHIRE
HEADS; LITTLE WOLF AND YELLER WOLF, ESQS

Dear Mum and Dad,

Just got your letter saying let him get on with it. Good because I have.

From your not so wurrid,
Little

Dear Mum and Dad,

Good thing Adventure Acad is snowproof.
Outside is all white, Yeller's worst thing. It made
his voice lose some of its loudness. He said to
me, "OH NO, LICKLE, NOW MISTER MARVO
WON'T COME! THE SNOW IS TERRIBLE!"

But he did, he came by snowmobile! It is a
big shiny one with a propeller behind. Plus
cosy glass cabin in front. Mister M is tall and
smart with his black coat sticking out at the
back and a big fuzzy beard. It comes right up to
his glinty eyes. His voice is a sleepy one and his
smell is like pepper and his eyebrows are red
and bristly.

After tea he showed me and Yeller some plans of Instant Adventures. He does nice curly capitals and he is a good colourinner. But plans are hard to understand for small cubs. Never mind, because Mister Marvo is so clever. He says, "Believe me, my boys, these are the most marvellous, most modernest adventures money can buy! They cost a lot, but remember, they are all under 1 winterproof dome. So you can have the thrills without the chills."

Yeller said, "ARRRROOOO! BECAUSE SNOW IS MY WORST THING, IT GIVES ME THE TREMBLES. BUT NOW, GUESS WHAT LICKLE, WE CAN HAVE A GO WITHOUT THE SNOW!!"

See what you are missing?

Yours xcitedly

L

Dear M and D,

Smells thinks Mister Marvo is brilliant. He has let him share his dorm, also shown him his ted and his safe even!

Me and Yeller are not jealous because now we can get on playing Bossy Heads and Daring Deeders by ourself. Important for the practiss. And tomorrow we choose our Instant Adventures, arrrroooo!

Yours thrilly,

Little

Dear Mum and Dad,

Plan plan plan is what me and Yeller and Mister Marvo are up to, phew. Smells will not help, he only likes counting gold.

These are our best IAs so far (short for Instant Adventures).

PIRATE RAIDERS

SPACE RANGERS

FIERCE FIGHTERS

NIGHT ON MONSTER MOUNTAIN

TARZAN ZIPWIRES

Mister Marvo said did we want BANGS-U-LIKE ADVENTURE which is like a forest? You creep through it and loads of pretend hunters jump out and shoot their guns at you. Yeller said "GOOD IDEA, I LOVE LOUDNESS."

But I said, "No, that is enough IAs for now."

I did not want to say I am v scared of bangs, but all of a suddenly, Mister Marvo said softly, "Look deep into my eyes, my boy, and tell me. Are bangs your worst thing?" Just then Yeller did a loud sneeze, lucky for me. It made me jump plus it stopped me giving away my secret.

So Mister Marvo said, "Well done, my boy, it is plain that you do not fear bangs. You are thinking of your pupils. They will not all be as fearless as you. By the way, the Instant Adventures you have selected will cost 3 wheelbarrowsful of gold, paid in advance."

I said, "What, before you build anything? Good joke har har."

Mister Marvo got quite snarly then. It made his beard slip a bit. But quick as a chick he hid his sharp teeth. And now he says he will build us a nice Example IA to show us his marvellous work. Not the big winterproof dome, because that goes on last. No, it is a mini TARZAN ZIPWIRE. Good, eh?

Yours,
Littly

Dear M and D,

Smells is still OK but a bit jealous and fidgety because of Mister Marvo doing planning with us. Yesterday he kept climbing on top of his safe and falling off. Just so we would stick plasters on him.

Then Yeller had a BIG IDEA. He made Smells a tape of gold going chinkle chinkle. Now it is 1 of his best things. He sits and listens to it all the time with his Walkwolf on.

See, we are looking after him still.

Your trusted
Little

27

Dear Mum and Dad,

Today Mister Marvo put up the mini Tarzan Zipwire in our dorm to show us.

I said to Yeller, "Yeller, what do you think?" He said to me, "I THINK IT IS A BIT RUBBISH, LICKLE." Mister Marvo said to Yeller, "With respect, my boy, Master Little is the true owner here. I advise you to keep silent." He gave Yeller a deep look in the eyes and guess what, Yeller said, "OF COURSE, MISTER MARVO." It is so hard to say no to Mister Marvo.

True the zipwire is a bit smaller than we hoped. More washingliney than Tarzanny. But still, we had 236 goes on it. It is good the way it makes your eyes water and blows your fur back. Also you go dong off the tyres at the end and that takes some daringness.

Mister Marvo says not to be wurrid, it is just an Example IA. When we pay him, he will build a huge big scary real 1 over a stream with pretend crocs going snap. Oo-er!

Yours phewly,

L

Dear Mum and Dad,

Sorry to hear about your blizzard blowing. Another white whisker day here also. So sleep well, see you in Springtime. Us cubs are much 2 busy for long zizzing.

Yes I will write down all news but not send it, just save it for when you wake up. I will put it all in my Daring Deed book that Yeller gave me. No I will not disturb, only in Emerjuncy. Like if any badness happens to my baby bruv. Which it will not, Dad, because yes I do remember what you get like when you go RAVING MAD.

Yours nightnightnightnightnightnightly ect (get it?),

L

Dear Hibernaties,

Mister Marvo is still here. He is doing lots of hard complications and guess what he says? He says, "My boys, you now have my personal guarantee as a marvoman and inventor, that your Instant Adventure Playground, the finest in the world, will be ready by the end of the month! My team of busy beavers will start work as soon as I give the word."

Arrrroooo! Time to get our pupils together. Must think up a good advert.

Yours thinkingly,
   Little

Dear Hiberzizzers,

Smells has gone barmy about Yeller's chinkle tape, he loves it, kiss kiss!

He has stopped talking to everybody. He only likes staying in his dorm guarding his safe, so he can count up gold, plus listening to his chinkle tape on his Walkwolf. I think Mister Marvo is a bit upset. He keeps saying "My boy, this won't do at all. Won't you look deep into my eyes and say 'Yes, Mister Marvo, I am your best pal?'" But Smells just turns up his Walkwolf and sings, "Chinkle chinkle little gold, you are wot I like to hold."

Yours reportingly,
L Wolf (Head)

~~OTTER~~ BALLOON,

↖ Hot air, sorry

above Frettnin Forest

Dear M and D,

Yeller has thought of an advert for getting pupils, it is just the best! That is Y I am writing this in a balloon!!! It has the shape of Adventure Acad, but with a basket hanging under.

Me and Yeller are floating over Frettnin Forest. We have got cardboard loudshouters and this is what we shout for our advert (Yeller made it up but I wrote it down):

"Ahoy ahoy, brute beasts!! Do you like adventures? Then come to our school and have some. Yes, come to Adventure Academy! It is the big place they used to call Cunning College. Mister Bigbad Wolf was the Head. But not now, he went off bang and died. So all is changed, no need to fear and fret. Little and Yeller Wolf are the new Heads. So come, be our pupils! Try our new adventure playground. It is the BEST FUN EVER! Plus you get Daring Deed Awards. Arrrooo!"

Yours skyhighly,
L

ADVENTURE ACADEMY

FRETTNIN FOREST, BEASTSHIRE
HEADS; LITTLE WOLF AND YELLER WOLF, ESQS

Dear Mum and Dad,

Bit wurrid about baby bruv again. It is gold gold gold all the time with him now.

I know you think he has not got goldfever. But last night he gave his precious ted a bath in gold! I fear he is a bit gone in the brane because everybody knows Smells hates baths.

Also, now he has locked Mister Marvo out of his dorm and will not speak to him at all.

Yours ahwelly,
Little

ADVENTURE ACADEMY

FRETTNIN FOREST, BEASTSHIRE
HEADS; LITTLE WOLF AND YELLER WOLF, ESQS

Dear Zizzy Parents,

I am writing this tucked up 2.

Good news, our balloon advert worked. Now we have got 1 pupil. He was left on our doorstep. He is a small crow with not much feathers, v shy with a label on. He does not say much, only Ark. This is what the label said:

STUBBS CROW
TOO FRIT TO FLY
BUT GOOD AT
BEAKWORK

Yours,

L Wolf (Head)

ADVENTURE ACADEMY

FRETTNIN FOREST, BEASTSHIRE
HEADS; LITTLE WOLF AND YELLER WOLF, ESQS

Dear Parents,

Some cubs would look at Stubbs and say, "Hmm nice snack", but not me and Yeller. We want to teach him not eat him.

Yeller is good at being a Head. He shouts cheery things like, "HELLO STUBBY! WELCOME TO ADVENTURE ACADEMY. ME AND MY CO-HEAD LICKLE WILL SOON TEACH YOU HOW TO BE A HIGH FLYER AND DARING DEEDER LIKE US. BEAK UP! NO NEED TO BE A SCAREDYCROW!"

Also we have let him nest in the fireplace in the hall with his head up the chimney to feel more homely.

Yours Headly,

L

ADVENTURE ACADEMY

FRETTNIN FOREST, BEASTSHIRE
HEADS; LITTLE WOLF AND YELLER WOLF, ESQS

Dear Parents,

Mister Marvo has finished his complications,
now he keeps asking and asking for 1 wheelbarrow
of gold at least. Just to start up, he says. It is hard
saying no to him but Yeller says we must try and
keep our firmness up, saying, "NO MEANS
NO!" with loud grrrs like Dad.

What I do if he talks softly to me is cross my
eyes and go blah doo dum diddle inside my head.

I just heard him going mumblymumbly up to
bed. I wish he would hurry up and bring his
busy beavers to start work on the Adventure
Playground, then he can have his gold.

Yours keentostartly,

L

ADVENTURE ACADEMY

FRETTNIN FOREST, BEASTSHIRE
HEADS; LITTLE WOLF AND YELLER WOLF, ESQS

Morning

Dear Mum and Dad,

Good thing I am writing this
in my Diary of Daring Deeds
and not posting this yet.
Because I think you might go
a bit mad.

It is just that Mister Marvo has stolen
all my gold and cubnapped Smells, sorry.

Your other boy,
    L Wolf

PS But do not get wurrid, by
the time you read this,
everything will be Ok.
Probly.

39

ADVENTURE ACADEMY

FRETTNIN FOREST, BEASTSHIRE
HEADS; LITTLE WOLF AND YELLER WOLF, ESQS

Later

Dear Mum and Dad,

Help, we still do not know what to do!
Because 1) the snow is tall as cubs, 2) Yeller is
scared of snow. Also how can we catch up
Mister Marvo in his fast snowmobile? Oo-er.

Just back from a clue hunt. Near the front
door we found:

1 top hat

1 bushy beard

1 long coat with red
tailhairs all up the back inside.

What do they mean?

Yours stumpedly,
Little

40

Much Later

Dear M and D,

Oh no, guess what, Mister Marvo is not really a marvoman and inventor at all! No, he is a cunning fox and a clever dizgizzer (cannot spell it). And his really truly name is Mister Twister the Fox! He was Uncle Bigbad's crime partner, remember? Also he made me work for

him at Borderlands Market 1 time when I was lost. Fancy me not knowing him by his pepper smell plus his sneaky questions like are bangs my worst thing? Plus saying MY BOY THIS and MY BOY THAT all the time!

WANTED

Mr. Twister (Fox)
HUGE REWARD

Smells left a clue too, but it is rubbish
because he can only do ABC. This is it:

Do not fret and fear, I spect Yeller will think
up a rescue Idea soon.

Yours onyourmarksly,
Little

Dear M and D,

The cheery news is we are on the trail of
Mister Twister on my bike (Yeller's idea, quicker
than paws). He has got the Snowtrembles v
bad. His voice has gone all quiet. This morning
he whispered to me, "LICKLE, THE SNOW HAS TOOK
MY VOICE."

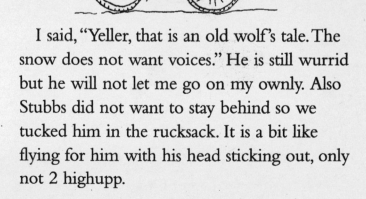

I said, "Yeller, that is an old wolf's tale. The
snow does not want voices." He is still wurrid
but he will not let me go on my ownly. Also
Stubbs did not want to stay behind so we
tucked him in the rucksack. It is a bit like
flying for him with his head sticking out, only
not 2 highupp.

We have plenty of snacks, tent, torches, ect.
Also Yeller has brought Smells' clue, plus his kite
with the yellow wolf eyes and strong string as
Rescue Kit. Now we are having a short rest in
a small gap in Frettnin Forest. 2 cold stars are
lighting this letter, maybe 3, brrr. I think we
have come 4 or 5 miles. If we keep on the
snowmobile track, fine. If not, whoops plop,
where are we? Answer, under the snow digging.

Yours searchingly,
   Little

PS We will rescue Smells quick as we
can, so Dad, do not go RAVING MAD.

Dear Mum and Dad,

What a rooty nightride we had through
Frettnin Forest with our torches going flash.
The tent was so heavy on the back of the bike,
also it pressed on the brakes and made us go
slower. But all is not sadness and sore botts
because we have got to the south shore of Lake
Lemming. Now v late but we can rest. The
tent is up and a snuggly fit with 3 of us in.

Yeller and me had hedgehog and cowparsley
soup for a warmupp. I said to Stubbs, "Do
crows like chocklit earwigs?" He said "Ark!
Ark-zactly!" his 1st words. He is a bit shy for
Rescue work.

Yours sorebottly,
L

45

Dear Mum and Dad,

I cannot sleep because of thinking Y did Mister Twister take Smells with him? Is it...

A) because he likes small pests or

B) because Smells loves gold so much he will not say the combination of the safe?

I bet it is B. And I bet when they are faraway, Mister Twister will take the Walkwolf off Smells's ears. Then he will say softly, "Look deep deep into my eyes, my boy, and tell me the number of your safe." Not fair, because Mister Twister is such a cunning crook and cubnapper but Dad will still go raving mad at *me* for letting a bad thing happen to Smells.

Your grumpy
Little

46

Dear Mum and Dad,

Yeller and me were all down and dumpy
after only a small zizz. I was on the back of the
bike because it was Yeller's turn to pedal. He
said whisperly, "PHEW LICKLE, THIS IS 2 HARD FOR
ME. I WISH THERE WAS A MORE EASY WAY TO CATCH
THAT SNOWMOBILE."

Just then Stubbs tapped me on the head and
pointed his beak northly. I said,
"Do you mean go
straightly, the crow
way?" He said,
"Ark." I said, "But
that is straight over
the lake." He said,
"Ark-zactly!".

But how to cross? The hard icelid on the lake
was 2 skiddy for bikers. Then I said wait, the
plastic picnic plates!

We got off the bike and Yeller and me tied 1
on each back paw. Then on to the lake we
stepped. "Hold tight, Stubbs!" I said and off we
went, skaty skate! 1st we went
FFFSHH-BONK, OO MY NOSE!
FFFSHH-BONK, OO MY TAIL!

But then Stubby spread out his wings for the
balance and off I sailed, smooth as smooth! That
gave Yeller the Idea to use his kite, so no more
falling down for us. Oo what a thrilly feeling
and FREEE! Better than silly old Tarzan

Zipwires that cost barrows of money! Also, a good Daring Deed for my Diary, tick. ✔

1 bad thing about picnic plates is they are brakeless. So we met the north shore in a sudden way. Lucky there was a soft snowpile to land in, phew.

We brushed ourselves off and guess what we saw right away, snowmobile tracks going hillward, arrrooo! So that Mister Twister better watch out, we know he has gone to Windy Ridge!

Yours sherlockly,
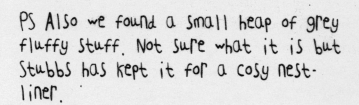
Little

PS Also we found a small heap of grey fluffy stuff. Not sure what it is but Stubbs has kept it for a cosy nest-liner.

Dear Mum and Dad,

After a short rest, we all did jumping for the warmness. Also made a fire for toasting cheese (Stubbs's best snack). Crunchy shrewbar for me, hmmm nice, then quickmarch, back doing Rescuing.

All afternoon we hiked pantingly. At last Stubbs tapped my head and then his beak pointed over the hill to Windy Ridge. Aha, there was the snowmobile right up there, with Mister Twister plus Smells tied up! Yeller said (small trembly voice), "LET'S CREEP UP CLOSE, LICKLE, THEN WAIT TILL DEEP DARK. THEN JUMP ON THAT FOX AND CAPTURE HIM!"

We got on our bellyfur in the cold snow, doing the wolfcrawl. Poor Yeller, it was so bad for his Snowtrembles. But Stubbs helped him keep up his cheeryness whispering, "Ark! Ark-cellent!

50

Ark–cellent!" all the way up to the top.

We waited and waited, quiet as catbreath till the dark was deep. Then one paw at a time, careful not to make the snow squeak:

We got out our torches

And we snuck up behind Mister Twister

And tied him up quick!

Only it was not Mister Twister, ect, only cardboard cutouts and a note.

My boys, you can never hope to catch me. It is only a matter of time before the Brat tells me the combination of the safe. Then I shall release him. So give up and go home. Otherwise you will put the Brat in danger and you will face some VERY LOUD BANGS. You have been warned. Give up now, signed Mister Twister.

Yours trickedly,
      Little

Dear Mum and Dad,

Today was just the worst. Mister Twister had tons of time to escape across the Dark Hills, plus get here to Broken Tooth Caves.

Before we started, Yeller said, "BANGS ARE YOUR WORST THING, LICKLE. DO YOU WANT TO GIVE UP?" I said, "Snow is your worst thing. Do you want to give up?" We both said, "No!" and kept going. So now Mister Twister will most probly join up with some outlaws in a gang and bash us.

The Dark Hills were v cold and horrible with snow coming down feathers. So no more snowmobile tracks. Then down flew that sharp stuff, not snow, more like grit or stingflies but no taste. Sleet is it?

This is a bad place. So many caves, all joined together like ratruns. Just the lurky sort that outlaws and bears like, oo-er!

We have picked a good dry cave for our nightlair. Hope we can keep safe.

Your tracky boy,
Little

Dear Mum and Dad,

Today we did a Daring Deed with a lion in it. Yes a real mountain 1!

We slept a safe night but boiling up bat soup for breakfast was 2 much of a danger-tempter. Because a hungry old mountain lion came sniffing! Stubbs smelt his catsmell before me even, and saved us from ambush. He went, "Ark! Ark-shun stations! Ark-shun stations!" We just had time to run behind the fire. All of a suddenly, we saw his eyes, then his teeth, then his blue cap and waistcoat. He went,

Stubbs whispered, "Ark! Ark-zaggerating," which I did not think so because of my ears ringing. But Stubbs flapped his short wings at the fire and puffed up the flames and smoke. And, do you know what, that lion was not as fierce as his roar. Because he started coughing and creeping away!

Then he tried to trick us with big stories then, saying, "Oy be a narsty ole RRRRobber ye know. And oy be a wicked ole RRRRRipper!"

Quick as a chick I said "Listen Mister Mountainlion, if you help us, maybe we can find a nice juicy mice pie or 3 for you, yes?"

No more snarls at all after that, just chew chew lipsmack lipsmack.

That is how we craftily found out:

1) a fox and small wolfcub stayed in a secret
   hideout cave last night

2) that same fox went HAR HAR about trick
   cutouts

3) that same fox said he was going to learn his
   map by heart and chew it up so nobody
   could follow

4) that same fox said to the small wolfcub about
   going across the border into Grimshire. To
   Hamneezia, the forgotten village.

Now guess who that fox and wolfcub are!!?

Yours aharly,
   Little

Dear Mum and Dad,

Stubbs woke us up today going, "Ark!
Ark-shun stations!" He was having a nightmare
about getting lost. That made me get wurrid
because of not having a map. But then I said,
"Quick, Yeller, pass me the string off your kite.
We are off to find the secret hideout cave where
Mister Twister and Smells spent the night!"

Off went Yeller and me
tunnelling. Stubbs stayed
outside with 1 end of the string
in his beak. Also I tied the other end to my tail.
It was twisty work, but with our torches going
flash and tugs on my tailstring from Stubbs, we
never got lost, not once!
We were hopeless
hunters for ages, then all
of a suddenly I got a
niff of baby bruvsmell.

"Arrrooo," I said. "This is it, the secret hideout cave!"

Yeller said, "YOU'RE RIGHT, LICKLE BECAUSE LOOK, BITS OF CHEWED MAP ALL OVER THE FLOOR!"

Just then I saw another clue, it was some more of that grey fluffy stuff like we found by Lake Lemming! We picked up the paper and the fluff, then I went tugtug on the string and Stubbs pulled me in like fishing. Outside in the daytime light I said, "Oh boo, this is not like maps, more like spilt ratflakes, now we will never find the way."

Stubbs said, "Ark! Ark-zammin, Ark-zammin!" meaning let me see. He tucked the fluff in with his other nest-liner in the rucksack. Then we found out why his label said he was good at beakwork. Because he got all the chewedupp bits of paper and stuck them together with spiderwebs. So arrrooo, we are mapless no more!

Northeast is the quick way to Hamneezia from here. Pity it is over the Grim Mountains, they are a bit 2 high for small crows scared of highness. Still, he says he will go for the Arksperience, brave eh? Hope he does not get 2 giddy.

Yours readysteadyly,
Little

Dear Mum and Dad,

Off early with Stubbs snugged down in the grey fluffy stuff at the bottom of my rucksack. 3 Grim Mountains ago I said to Yeller, "I hate this high land, it is 2 hard on paws."

But up Mount Tester we went struggling. So slippy, but then we found new tricks for climbing. Plus Stubbs kept saying a muffly "Ark! Ark-cellent!", meaning well done. Mount Tester was a hard tester for climbing (get it?), hard up the south side, hard down the north side.

Then came Mount Skyward, about the same. But half way up Mount Farview it got 2 steep, the cliff started leaning out over us! I was keeping up with Yeller nearly, but all of a suddenly I lost my pull. I could not go up, I could not go down. My trembles made Stubbs pop out to look. I said, "No Stubbs! 2 highupp for you! Stay inside the rucksack!"

But he would not, he struggled out saying,
"Arks Arks!"

I said, "Ice axe? Where?" and he gave me
a small peck on the head. I said, "Your
beak?" And that was what he meant.

So I took a trusting hold of his twiggy
legs and UP I swung him. Then I gave a
loud arrrooo for the best beak I know!
Because it stuck in the ice like a bee's
stinger in a bear's nose!

And that was how Yeller, Stubbs and me
climbed the highest harshest mountain in
Beastshire. All on our ownly we would be
dead now. But together, slow but sure, we
have done a Daring Deed like no cub or
crowlet has ever done before. So into the
Diary of Daring Deeds it goes, tick. ✓

Now we are the high-uppest campers
in Beastshire.

Yours daringly,
L Wolf

Hamneezia,
Grimshire

Dear Mum and Dad,

Which was our worst, climbing down from Mount Farview or crossing the rope bridge over Perilus Pass? Answer, the bridge, because mountains are cold and crool but they do not wobble. Also rope bridges try to tip you off, AHHHHEEEeeee splosh! into roary water with sharp rocks sticking up. So that is enough writing about Perilus Bridge, it was bad as bangs nearly.

So I will say about Hamneezia. We got here after dark with snow floating down, v frozz and gloomy and glum. Nobody here remembers a snowmobile coming, they just forget everything.

Yours brrrly,

L

Dear M and D,

That Hamneezia was bad for branes, it made you feel giveuppish. So we ran off quick next day. Now we are in Spooke where the silver miners live. It is quite nice if you like old huts and piles of rubble everywhere.

There is 1 good game they have here. It is called Hello Ween and it is like this. 1st you must have some gloomyness and pumpkins with candles in, yum, tasty! Next what you do is, you dress up like a witch or ghosty or skerlington (cannot spell it). Then you walk up and down the street going woo. Then you go up to a door, knockknock. Then you say, "TREACLE TRICK!!" And you get given yummy snacks to eat!

Yeller said, "COR, LICKLE, OUR PUPILS WILL LOVE THIS! LET'S BUY SOME BOGIEBEAST MASKS WITH GREEN GLOWPAINT ON. THEN WE CAN TEACH HELLO WEEN AT ADVENTURE ACADEMY." So we bought loads.

Tonight we are having a nice cosy curl-up. We want to get our strongness up for rescuing Smells.

3 woos from
Little

Dear M and D,

Oh no, Yeller is in bed with his tremblyest Snowtrembles ever! Here is the story of Y.

We were asking and asking for clues about Mister Twister but in a hopeless way. Then, nice surprise, we came to Bodger Badger's Garage and a cheery badger working there. I said, "Have you seen a snowmobile, a big shiny one with a propeller behind?"

The badger said,
"Oo arr. Lemmy see.
Oo arr. Snowmobile?
Yerss, me dears.
Stopped by here 3 days
ago, oo arr. Nice old
lady driver there was.
Her hair was whoyt as
snow. She asked me to fix on an extra big fuel tank, yerss she did.

And she bought an extra-strong roofrack and all. She had this big heavy iron box, oo arr. That took up too much room in the cabin, see?"

Stubbs said, "Ark! Ark-straordinary!"

I said, "Was there a small smelly wolfcub with this old lady?"

The badger said, "Dunno about no wolfcub, oo arr. She had her baby grandson with her, but I never did see his face. Poor thing, he had the chickypox. So his granny had to wrap him up tight all over ter stop him scratchin, see? Looked loik a little Egyptian mummy he did, oo arr."

I said, "But was he very squeaky and wiggly?"

The badger said, "Ooo arr! Ever so squeaky and wiggly!"

I said, "I think I know that squeaky baby. And did the old lady smell of pepper by any chance?"

Answer, "OOOOO ARRR!!"

"AND WHICH WAY DID THEY GO?" asked Yeller.

Answer, northeast towards Yellowsmoke. "But oo arr, you don't want to go there on foot, me dears," said the badger. "Not across the White Wildness. There be no roads to follow, you know, nor no shelter. Just blizzards brewing. The worstest snowyest place on earth, that is."

That was when Yeller fainted. Now he is tucked up tight in Bodger Badger's spare room. Maybe he will feel better tomorrow.

Yours lettshopingly,
L Wolf

Dear Mum and Dad,

Stubbs and me have gone on alone. We miss Yeller a lot. But he was 2 ill to come with us. Also he feels much shame to be a giveupper.

But I said, "Never mind, Yeller, some beasts do not like high places, some beasts do not like bangs. You WISH you were just normal and untrembly but you are not, so there."

I am writing sadly in a snowhole in the White Wildness. It is true about the whiteness, it is all white here, even the bears.

So no more now from
Little Wolf

Dear Mum and Dad,

Brrrrrr, so frozz, so weak.

Stubbs says all crows are Arksperts on going the quick way. That is why everybody says "It is 2 miles as the crow flies ect." Except Stubbs of course, he hates flying. Anyway, he says we are going northeast.

But I am not so sure. I have run and run today. But Yellowsmoke is not near.

I have dug a snowcave.

2 cold 2 write more,

L

snowcave,
white wildness

Dear M and d,

So tired   sore eyes   blizzard bad   trapped in snowcave

no food today   just lick snow   zizz   wake

sometimes I send up my Emerjuncy Howl for the wind to carry

But I am getting 2 weak

we have put out Yeller's kite to fly for a signal Also Stubbs has done plaiting the string for strongness

the wolfeyes on it shine   but who will see?

From
    L W

drear mumdad, I cannot stay wakey only

dream of monster big growler

coming   closer   closer

Dear Mum and Dad,

Phew days since I wrote to you, sorry, it was the weakness.

About my dream, it was not a dream. It was the Snowmonster crawled into our snowcave. To take us away. Shiny blue body, blue head and buggy eyes. He was a terror but he came whisperingly. He did not roar, do you know Y?

Because he was not the Snowmonster, he was YELLER!!

He was wearing Bodger Badger's blue snowsuit! Off came his helmet and goggles and earmuffs. And there was his funny pointy face and his stickyout teeth, laughing. His voice is still not back to normal loudness, but even whispery it

72

makes you laugh. He said, "SORRY TO KEEP YOU WAITIN. ANYBODY WANNA NICE FIGHT?"

I said ME! and over and over we rolled, the happiest wrestlers ever! It was a bit hot and squashy for small crows but soon Stubbs forgot shyness and joined in with some good rough pecks. That night we had a newsy Togetheragain Feast with yummy stuff from Bodger's larder. Rabbit rolls and mice pies for me and Yeller, hmmm yes please. And Stubbs had his faves, worms on toast and crawlycake.

I will say Yeller's news in my next.

Yours togetherly,

$$ \Psi\Psi + \dot{\Psi} + L $$

Dear M and D,

Here is Yeller's story. He told it like this.

"WELL LICKLE AND STUBBY, THAT TIME YOU WEN AWAY, I
FELT SHOCKIN. I FELT SHAMED. I FELT THE LONEST
WOLFCUB IN THE LAND. I KEP THINKIN 'I MUST HELP MY
CHUMS'. BUT EVERY TIME I GOT OUT OF BED I THOUGHT
OF THE WHITE WILDNESS. AND I JUST FELL ON MY FACE,
FLOP – LIKE THAT. I COULDN'T STOP FAINTIN, NOT WITH
THE TREMBLES SO SHOCKIN.

THEN ONE LONE NIGHT I HEARD SOMETHIN CALLIN ME.
IT WAS COMIN DOWN MISTER BODGER'S CHIMNEY.
FARAWAY LIKE, BUT STILL CLEAR AS WATER. I SAYS TO
MESELF "THAT'S LICKLE'S EMERJUNCY HOWL, THAT IS! HE
WOULDN'T USE THAT IF HE WASN'T IN A DREADFUL BAD
WAY!' SO UP I JUMPS, CALLING, 'MISTER BODGER, MISTER
BODGER! YOU'VE GOT TO HELP ME SAVE LITTLE WOLF AND
STUBBY CROW FROM DEATH BY BLIZZARDS!'

HE SAYS TO ME, 'ARE YOU UP TO IT?' I SAYS 'I'VE GOT TO
BE!'

SO DOWN WE WENT TO THE GARAGE. MISTER BODGER
GOT A BIG OLD MOTORBIKE, PLUS A BIG WHEEL OFF OF A
TRACTOR, PLUS A SLEDGE. AND HE JOINED UM ALL UP
TOGETHER WITH SPANNERS. AND BEFORE MORNING CAME
HE MADE ME A SPEEDY SNOWTORBIKE! THEN HE GAVE ME
HIS OLD BLUE SNOWSUIT AND GOGGLES, A BIT BIG FOR ME
BUT GOOD FOR GETTIN MY BRAVENESS UP."

I said, "But still, how could you follow us?
Our tracks were covered up quick! So how?"

"Ark! Arksplain!" said Stubbs.

Answer, "THAT CLEVER CLUE FROM SMELLS!!"

I said, "Clever? Do you mean that screwedupp paper with the wobbly C plus splodge plus yellow scribbles like this?"

"WELL, LICKLE," said Yeller, "I FOUND OUT IT WAS NOT JUST SMELLS'S NORMAL DUNCENESS. NO, IT WAS A CRAFTY CLUE MEANING

C (SEE) YELLOW SMOKE!!"

So Yellowsmoke Swamplands is what Yeller aimed his snowtorbike at. And true the snow was a terror to him but he made the engine roar back at the blizzard. And at last he saw wolf eyes shining in the sky, and he thought, "I KNOW THAT KITE. I WILL SEE WHO IS ON THE END OF THE STRING!"

And he looked. And it was us, the end.
Another Daring Deed for my book! ✔
Arrooooo.

Yours savedly
   L

PS Now we can rescue Smells, let's hope
he is still ok, eh?

Dear Mum and Dad,

Fast riding makes you say to walking, "You
are just a slow snail!" But oh for a snowsuit plus
woolly helmet to stop cold ears!

Stubbs has got his grey fluffy stuff in the
rucksack for cosyness. But I had to sit behind
Yeller and hold tight. WISHWASH over
snowbumps and cracks we speeded. We went so
quick that now the Shivery Sea is just a short
twinkling away. Going WAAAAAH! was a big
help. But not having a
woolly helmet, my face
soon got frozz and my
WAAAAAH! got
stuck. When we
stopped, I could not
move, my mouth
looked like a
postbox for polar bears.

Lucky they have hot steamers in this land, they are like yellow smoke coming up out of the ground. Yeller and Stubbs had to lift me off the snowtorbike seat like a cardboard cutout and sit me in a steamer. Phew, goodbye frozz, hello warmalloverness plus my mouth going Yum Yum again for eating practiss!

Camping here tonight. Do not get wurrid, we will soon capture Mister Twister. And get Smells back, boo shame (only kidding, I miss him really).

Yours,

Dear M and D,

Oo-er hot steamers are a danger when they get big as trees. You have to go along a wiggly path to miss them. But it is a hard 1 to stay on. So Yeller drove slow and Stubbs and me were sharp lookouts. But sometimes, oh no, missed the path! Then WHOOOSH... up we went like a pingpong ball on a waterjet and BONK, down in the squidgy mud. No wonder flying is scary for Stubbs.

At last we have found the Shivery Sea, phew. It is grey and cold, like a big lake but more wavy. Plus it has pointy blue ice islands floating in it. Up we went northly along the beach searching searching.

But not 1 clue about Mister Twister boo shame.

Yours,

L

Dear M and D,

South again by snowtorbike along the beach.
Snow stopped but still no foxy tracks.

But clever old Stubbs spotted some grey
fluffy stuff, then a bit more, and a bit more! It
led to a rowboat full of holes. And in the sand
right nextdoor to the rowboat was a BIG
boatprint, plus scrape marks down to the sea.

Yeller looked on the floor of the rowboat.
"OH NO!" he whispered. "SHOCKIN!" His fur was
standing up on his neck. Because lying there,
flat like a cowpat, was a small body.

All I could say was Gulp.

Yours dreadly,
Little

Dear M and D,

Good news! That cowpat was not Smells! It was his ted with all the stuffing gone.

I am so proud of my baby bruv, even if he is a moany little scrooger. Unpicking his ted and dropping lumps of stuffing out of it for us to follow was a wolfly thing to do. Foxes think they know all the best tricks, so har har Mister Twister you never thought of that 1!

Spent today being boat fixers, maybe for a nice shelter. Also we had a good chat, so now we think we know where Mister Twister has gone with Smells.

Yeller said, "I THINK MISTER TWISTER HAD A BIG BOAT HERE. BIG ENOUGH FOR A SNOWMOBILE PLUS A SAFE, LICKLE. AND NOW HE HAS GONE SAILIN THE SHIVERY SEA."

But where xactly? Together we have made a strong new skin for the boat, with flatted out mudguards plus sledge bits off the snowtorbike. We buried the other bits. Also we have made oars out of tentpoles and picnic plates. Yeller's kite makes a hansum sail.

Your fixy boy,
L

PS Just now some crawly things came sideways out of the sea, and tried to pinch us with their pinchers. Handy, because it was tea time yum yum. Bit 2 much salt on them but nice and crunchy.

Dear M and D,

Today we lunched? lawnched? the boat.

We pushed it in the water, brrr frozz, so toes crossed for not sinking. It floated! I said, "You say a name for this boat, Stubbs." So Stubbs gave it the name *Ark*, just the job.

Sailing *Ark* was v scary, a bit 2 hilly for wolf cubs. But not Stubbs. He stood on the pointy bit at the front of the boat being the captain. Ups and downs did not bother him. I think it is a bit like flying but safe. His feathers are more bendy and black now, also shiny.

Me and Yeller did fast rowing to take our minds off sickupps. That puffs you out quick! Then all of a silently, up popped some nice nosy sea creatures, smooth as otters. Seals is their name, have you heard of it? We said our names 2 and told them about hunting for a cubnapper.

1 of the seals barked up, "Well mateys, all hands on deck and hoist your mainsail. Because we spied a big boat 4 tides ago. She was bound for Vile Island."

"Vile Island?" I said.

"Ark! Arksplain," said Stubbs.

"That's easy, me hearties," said the seal. "Vile Island is bang in the middle of the Shivery Sea."

Now the seals are giving us a tow, so must stop, 2 joggy 2 write.

Your queezy boy, Little

PS Just a short riddle, what makes Yeller green? Answer blue, also boats (hard 1, eh?)

Dear Mum and Dad,

Dry land, I love it kiss kiss, even if it is all boring rocks.

The seals towed us all the way here. We went skimming past lots of blue ice islands (seals call them iceburglars, I do not know Y). They were all jumpy with penguins.

At last we saw Vile Island, it is a sort of a big black pile of rocks with a castle on top. And now we are on it (the island not the castle). So 1 more Daring Deed for my book, tick. ✔

Now I will tell you a proud thing about Smells. Yeller says he has been thinking about my small bruv's clue. It was a much more crafty 1 than we thought before even.

Do you remember that wobbly C with the yellow smudges next to it like this?

Well it was not a wobbly C but a SHIVERY SEA! Get it?!! It was a small clue with a BIG meaning like this.

"Mister Twister is taking me to Vile Island next to the Yellowsmoke Swamplands in the middle of the Shivery Sea!"

Who would think a small brane like Smells's has got room for paper clues PLUS trails of tedstuffing? Must stop now. Yeller has thought of an idea for getting inside the castle. Now we can really start rescuing!

Small brane

Yours herewegoly,
L

Dear M and D,

Um, we have found Smells but we have been sort of um trapped everlastingly.

1 good thing yesterday was a new word I learnt, "dungeons". Dungeons are what you fall down trapdoors into when you go creeping about in castles. Otherwise my news is rubbish. We have been foiled by that foul foxy tricker, boo grrr.

We were all going ow and rubbing our botts, then all of a suddenly, down came a peppery smell. We looked up and wayupp above, sharp eyes were looking down. Shiningly through the trapdoor. Next came a soft foxy chuckle and words. "Good evening, my boys, congratulations. I underestimated you. No one has ever found my secret hideout before. And now, welcome to my deepest darkest dungeon. Please pay attention while I gloat."

"You see, my boys, you have fallen quite literally into my trap. You can never escape. Smellybreff has proved, shall we say, difficult? My softest voice is wasted on him and he is too fond of gold to give in to rough threats. So now it is up to you, my boys. Either persuade the little brat to give me the combination of the safe, or you will remain here for ever. Here he comes now. Do try to talk some sense into him, won't you?"

Down came a cat basket dangling. Smells was inside with a gag on.

Then BANG went the trapdoor. Just to make me tremble, I bet.

Your shaky boy,

L

Dear Mum and Dad,

Still trapped everlastingly, boo shame, and Mr Twister has pulled Smells up out of the dungeons again. We just had time to say praising things like Good clues, Smells, you are a Daring Deeder, keep chinnupply, keep saying nothing, ect. Then he was gone again going mmmm mmm through his gag.

1 problem. If Smells keeps saying nothing about combinations, Mister Twister will get his temper up, I bet. Good thing you are zizzing while these shocking adventures are happening to Smells and Me.

PS By the way, Stubbs wants me to write that he is holding my torch while I am doing this writing. So thanks Stubbs, nice beakwork.

Dear Mum and Dad,

Mister Twister came back to
speak to us this morning but not
with his temper up, phew. Only
for a goodbye gloat boo grr. He says he has found
a new way to make Smells be his friend again!

Because last night he told Smells a wopping fib.
That he will let him be King of Beastshire! He
says he can be on telly a lot, and all his subjects
must give him their gold to put in his safe.
Adventure Acad can be his palace and he can wear
a twinkly crown and boss everybody about, even
me and Yeller.

That fox is such a tempter. Now Smells will tell
him the combination I bet!

And we will be in the dungeons forevermore.

Yours howlingly,

L

Dear M and D,

We just heard Mister Twister's boat leaving, oh no! We have tracked him all this way to save Smells, now we must get back quick to Adventure Acad to save him. But how?

What shall I do? My Emerjuncy Howl will not reach you at the Lair. Plus no post box near! How can I wake you up? Now who will go RAVING MAD at Mister Twister and save Smells from his power? How can we ever escape from this deep dark dungeon???

Ah wait, Yeller has just looked at me thinkingly. Quick, I must lend him my pencil. Toes crossed he has got an idea that wants writing down.

Yours rushingly,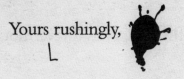
    L

Dear Mum and Dad,

Arrrroooo! Yeller's idea was an escaping 1! So here is the story of the Daring Deed that got us out of the dungeons, a good 1 for my diary, tick. ✔

Yeller said, "QUICK, STUBBY, STAND ON LICKLE'S HEAD. GOOD. NOW, LICKLE, STAND ON MY HEAD. THAT'S IT. NOW STUBBY, TIME FOR SOME CLEVER BEAKWORK. TRY PICKIN THE LOCK ON THE TRAPDOOR!"

Stubbs fainted 2 times because of highness, otherwise easy peas. The next hard part was climbing out, but arrrrooo again for the Rescue Kit kite string, so handy!!

Off we went quick down to the seashore. But too late, that nasty Mister Twister had burnt our boat!

Your marrowed boy (or is it macarooned?),

L B Wolf

Dear M and D,

Just a quick note but you will think, hmmm, interesting.

Being macarooned on Vile Island, we thought stuckly, ah well, what do rocky islands have for snacks? So we did rockpool hunts. We caught tickly things swimming like small commas with whiskers. They are v tasty, and the chewy stars. Also the flat crunchy things with pinchers we tried before, lots of those. Plus we liked the clingy things tucked up in their shells. Lucky Stubbs having a beak, much quicker than noses.

Then something happened. Like howling, but shivery and strange. Yeller found a broke drainpipe. He put 1 end into the water and said, "LICKLE, STUBBY, LISTEN DOWN THIS."
The sound was sea creatures calling. I put my mouth to the pipe and called ARRROooOOOOOOooo!

Back came a call AYEEEEEEEOOOEE.

What can it be?
L

Dear M and D,

Today I arrroooed down the pipe again and guess what, all of a suddenly black islands grew in the sea, 12, maybe more. They spouted water like Yellowsmoke steamers!

Then they swam right up to us in a pack. The leader put his wide flat chin on our beach and spoke low. "Who calls for a ride across the whaleroad?" His mouth was big enough to swallow a snowmobile.

"D-d-do you mean a ride across the sea?" I said all trembly.

"That is not the whale name. To us it is the whaleroad," said the packleader. "Our backs are at your service."

Down came his tail for us, a mighty 1 like a ramp. The other whales made a line in front of him. Stubbs hopped into my rucksack, Yeller gave a nod. And off we went across the whaleroad, running running till we crossed the Shivery Sea and reached the shore of Grimshire.

Yours puffed-outly
L

PS Big ✔ for a brilliant DD!

Dear M and D,

Still puffed out today and now camping yawnly not far from the River Riggly.

Whaleroad running was hard yesterday, also, quickmarching southly today. We must save Smells, he does not know what a tricker that fox is! So come on, Hazardous Canyon, we must get to you quick!!

Your racy boy,

L

Dear M and D,

We are so lucky having Stubbs, he may be just a small scaredycrow but also he keeps being a saver.

We looked and looked for bridges across the Riggly but no luck. So we thought ah well, cross it by log, here's one, paddle paddle. But no, that river was quick as a zipwire. *Zoooooom!!* we went, like a twig in a gutter. The rocks were sharp as teeth, lucky we missed them all, and on and on we went rushing, frozz and frit and tight clingers. Then we heard such a ROARING. We thought, Oh no, Funder Falls! Will we go H!
E!
L!
P!

splattt

Answer, nearly but no. Yeller said, "QUICK,
STUBBY, HELP ME WITH THE KITE. WE MUST SEND IT UP INTO
THE TREES TO TANGLE!"

Stubbs was doing his fastest beakwork
on the cross-sticks then WHOOSH!
ARRKK, come back, Stubbs!
Too late, up he went *swoosh* right
to the top of a tall oak tree.

Yeller and me held tight on the string
and went heave till we came to shore
at last, phew.

We got Stubbs down then, a bit trembly
but not hurt. We kept saying, "Gosh
thanks Stubbs, that was a Daring Deed
Stubbs, saved our lives Stubbs, you
really flew there Stubbs!"

Stubbs just said a shy, "Ark!
Ark-zaggerate!" Meaning that was not
real flying. So modest.

Yours dryingoffly,
L

Dear M and D,

Yesterday poor old Stubbs woke up sneezy, saying, "Ah-ah-Arkscuse! Ah-ah-Arkscuse!" But no time for bed and glowworm gargle, we must rush to save Smells.

So big problem at Hazardous Canyon. There is a notice there. It says

Yeller said, "LICKLE, I KNOW THIS IS A SHORTER WAY THAN GOIN OVER THE DARK HILLS TO LAKE LEMMIN. ALL THAT SNOW UP THERE, IT MIGHT FALL ON US."

I said, "Yes I know and it might make a big bang."

101

Then Stubbs went, "Ah–ah–ah–
ARKSCUSE!!!"

So Bang Rumble Splat down pounced an
avalanche on us.

Yours stifflocatedly,

L Wolf

Dear M and D,

Shhh, we are secretly camping in Frettnin
Forest. Cor, escaping from avalanches is hard. I
was so proud of Yeller, he hates even touching
snow. But Stubbs cawed, "ARK!
ARKSCAVATE!" meaning no time for
trembling, just hurry up and do tunnelling!

4 hours it took by hard claw and beakwork,
no rest no snacks, nothing. But then out we
tunnelled blinkingly into the moonshine. And
pant pant arrroooo for our good old Lake
Lemming, and watch out Mister Twister you
cubrobber! Because 3 Daring Deeders are
coming to get you!

Yours nearly homely,

L

Dear Mum and Dad,

Back at last BUT terrible news, the
Adventure Academy sign has gone. Now the
sign says,

Also we found chalky X marks on trees
everywhere! Why does he want to cut them
down? What is that Mister Twister up to?

Your wurrid

L

Dear M and D,

Adventure Acad has got all new big locks and bars on. So up we crept peepingly to the kitchen window. And guess what we spied, Smells gagged up and strapped in his highchair! Plus all the gold on the kitchen table being chinkled gloatingly by A BIG SNEAKY FOX, BOOO.

Not fair, Smells was 2 easy to tempt being just a titch. He told the combination, just to be a king and a star on telly. And he never got his twinkly crown even, so crool.

But what can we do to uncapture him? Mister Twister has got loads more cunningness than us, plus all the doors and windows locked tight.

Yours hinderedly,
L

Dear M and D,

Attacked at midnight!!

Mister Twister saw us doing spying, so he tried to kill us dead in our tent!

We thought we were tucked up safely in our secret camp. But no, BOOM!!! BANG!! my worst terror!! Down came fireballs falling slow, SCREAMING worse than owls. So bright! Even eyes shut did not stop you seeing

blue fireballs BANG

red fireballs BANG

green fireballs BANG

orange fireballs BANG

BANG!!!

I forget most of it now. Except rolling in the snow coldly. Then running running, more like a scaredy hen than a proud wolfcub. Then all was blackness. Then 2 wurrid pointy faces close to mine. Stubbs said, "Ark! Ark-splosion! Ark! Ark-cident!"

Yeller said, "HE FIREWURKED US, LICKLE. YOU BUMPED YOUR HEAD ON A TREE BUT YORE SAFE NOW."

I said, "Oh dear, sometimes I think Mister Twister is just 2 clever for us. What do you think?"

Yeller said, "GRRRRR. I THINK ENUF IS ENUF."

Yours shockedly,
L Wolf

Dear Mum and Dad,

Yeller has thought of an ABCD plan. We have done A nearly. Which is, bending back small trees all round Adventure Academy. Also tying them down with string, then loading them up with snowlumps (like catapults, get it?!).

It was so hard and such a danger because of Mister Twister on the roof. If he sees us just twitch, he shoots rockets at us! He is a deadly aimer and he knows bangs are my worst terror. But I did not run away henly. I must be a brave Arksample to Stubbs. Because of Plan B tomorrow.

Dear M and D,

Tonight is up to Stubbs.

Yeller has told him Plan B. Plus he has done a banner to get his braveness up.

ON THIS NIGHT
WITH NO HELP
FROM HOT STEMERS
OR KITES
   THE GRATE
STUBBY CROW
   WIL FLY

(Toes crossed for no fainting.)

Yeller and me are waiting in our hollow hidytree, ready for a fast race to the back wall of Adventure Acad, then tunnel quick into the cellar without Mister Twister seeing.

Stubbs is round the front now doing his job, keeping Mister Twister's sharp eyes off us. Catapult trees are ready all round, bended back and loaded with snowlumps.

So Plan B, you are on your marks. Stubbs the Crow, you must fly! Please fly Stubbs PLEEEEZ, you can do it.

This could be my last letter I bet. But you can still say "Oh well we are proud of Little and Yeller, because they did not half try to save our darling baby ~~pest~~ pet."

Farewell from

L B Wolf

Dear M and D,

We are IN secretly and that is 1 big tick for PLAN C, tunnelling! ✔ Yeller and me did tunnelling like 2 moles with a ferret chasing, phew pant. But question. Is Stubbs still a scaredycrow or a hero also? Answer, you will soon find out.

Plan B started with me doing my torchflash, our secret signal for Stubbs to fly quick and snip the catapult strings with his clever beak. But oh no! Mister Twister saw him doing his taxirun for takeoff. He loudshouted from the roof, "You foolish fledgling, you will never leave the ground! Take that!" Then he shot a big rocket right at him WEEEBOOM then more and more! Yeller and me thought, Oh no, he has exploded our cheery chum!

But then arrrooooOOOOOOOM!! LIFT OFF!!

Up went Stubbs faster than the rockets. He caught 2 of them in midair and pointed them back at Mister Twister going SCREEE-BLAMM! on to the roof. Arrooooo! that gave Mister Twister a sparky taste of his own shocks har har!!

.Plus he was so busy dancing on top of the house, he missed us doing Plan C, busy digging down the bottom!

Now we must wait here quiet as slugs. Before we can do PLAN D.

Yours shhhly,

L

PS Good thing we did tunnelling practiss at Hazardous Canyon, eh?

cellar
Adv Acad

Dear Mum and Dad,

Da-dah, we have rescued Smells! Because Mister Twister has locked himself in the belltower to stop being bombed by snow and his own rockets. So in we crept to the kitchen and untied the small wiggler.

I spect you are really really happy and grateful now, saying Arrooooo for our Daring Rescue Boy, ect. But Smells did not even say 'Thank you brave bruv'. All he did was he bit me, just for taking his gag off. How did I know he likes going mmm mm mmm? Also guess what, now he says he wants to be a cubnapper like Mister Twister. We have to let him tie us up all the time or he howls his head off. And the

113

worst thing, he has locked all the gold in the safe again and forgotten the combination!!

Mister Twister thinks we are still outside. We can hear him loudshouting to us from the belltower. Saying things like, "I know you are out there, my boys! But leave Frettnin Forest immediately. You will never stop me turning it into a Safari Park. Tomorrow my beavers begin cutting down trees to make room for the motorway. And in no time the hunters will be here with their loud guns. So BANG BANG you will be shot!"

Oo-er, better hurry up and do Plan D! We need some dressing up for it, also some cooking smells to tempt that fox down from the belltower.

So loads to do before midnight.

Your busy boy,

L

Dear M and D,

All set for Plan D and only 1/2 past 11, so time for a small note to say about it.

Yeller and me have got all our stuff ready:

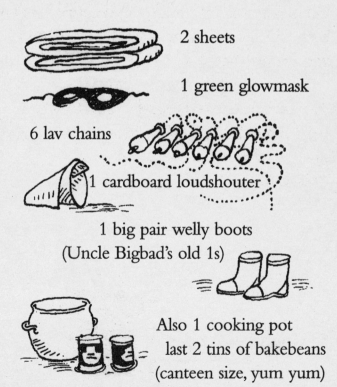

2 sheets

1 green glowmask

6 lav chains

1 cardboard loudshouter

1 big pair welly boots
(Uncle Bigbad's old 1s)

Also 1 cooking pot
last 2 tins of bakebeans
(canteen size, yum yum)

Just before midnight we will cook the bakebeans. Up will go the lovely smell. Down will come Mister Twister drool drool. Then out behind the curtain will come Yeller dressed up as a Bogiebeast. Also I will do a scary voice like this:

I AM THE GHOST OF BIGBAD WOLF

FLY AND FLEE FOUL FOX!!

SHOVE OFF TO VILE ISLAND

AND STAY THERE.

AND IF YOU BLINKING BLUNKING DON'T

I'LL BOIL UP YER WICKED BONES

AND SERVE YER UP AS SOUP!

Then Mister Twister will go oo-er mercy and run off. Good eh?

Yours craftily,

L

Dear M and D,

Plan D went a bit wrong, this is how.

The cooking part was good. Up went the bakebeany whiff, tempt tempt. Then down the belltower steps came Mister Twister drool drool. Smells was in his highchair, pretending to be tied up still. I was hiding under the table, also Yeller was hiding behind the curtain dressed up as a Bogiebeast.

In came Mister Twister quickmarch towards the cooking pot. In went the ladle, stir stir lipsmack lipsmack. I thought come on Yeller, hurry up, start shocking!

Then guess what, Yeller did not come through the curtains, he came through the wall! And he did not have his glowmask on, he had a big furry face instead, plus great big red eyes

and great big yellow teeth, plus all dribble
dribbling down. Plus his eyebrows met in the
middle like 2 furry caterpillars. Plus he looked
all tall and thin and horrible.

Also he did not let me say my scary words,
he did his own ones like this:

I AM THE GHOST OF UNCLE BIGBAD!

ME WOT DIED OF THE JUMPING BEANBANGS!

I DROOL, I DROOL FOR A LUVLY GOBFULL!

FETCH ME THE SHOVEL AND FEED ME SWIFTLY!

Mister Twister went white as a polar bear
and jumped straight out of the window.

So I said, "Cor, Yeller, you were brilliant. You
have scared Mister Twister away for ever I bet."

Only it was not Yeller. Yeller came out
through the curtains in his Bogiebeast outfit.
So I said, "Well who is that with the big red
eyes and yellow teeth and all dribble dribbling
down?"

And Yeller looked

       and he saw

         and he went

AAAAAAAAAAaaaaaaaaaaaaaa!!

And so did I.

Yours oo-erly,

    L Wolf

Adventure Academy

FRETTNIN FOREST, BEASTSHIRE
HEADS; LITTLE WOLF AND YELLER WOLF, ESQS

Dear M. and D,

Arrrroooo, Mister Twister is really gone. And 3 arrroooos for Stubbs! Because just as Mister Twister jumped out the window, guess who came flying through? Answer Stubbs the Crow! What a flyer, he loves it! He says it is Ark! Ark! Ark-zillerating!

Me and Yeller and Smells had all our fur up with scaryness when he flew in. He said, "Ark! Ark-straordinary!" meaning you lot look like you have seen a ghost. Which we had. Fancy Uncle Bigbad coming back from the nice grave I dug for him, eh? I spose he came back for a shovelful of bakebeans, he was always keen.

Good fun though eh?

Yours cheerily,
Littly

Dear Mum and Dad,

It is sooooo nice Yeller having his old noisy voice back. It was the shock did it for him.

We have been talking and talking about Adventure Acad. Yeller said, "KNOW WHAT I THINK, LICKLE, I THINK INSTANT ADVENTURE PLAYGROUNDS ARE FOR TAME PETS, NOT FOR BRUTE BEASTS LIKE US."

I said, "Yes, we like getting our braveness up in wild places, don't we?"

Yeller said, "LET'S NOT TEACH DARING DEEDS. LET'S HAVE ANOTHER SORT OF SCHOOL."

I said, "Good idea, but let us have a 1st Prize Day for our best pupil!"

Stubbs said a happy Ark! Ark-zackly! and did a loopheloop round the light.

Yours,

L

ADVENTURE ACADEMY

FRETTNIN FOREST, BEASTSHIRE
HEADS; LITTLE WOLF AND YELLER WOLF, ESQS

Prize Day

Dear Mum and Dad,

Today us Heads awarded our pupil Stubbs Crow the Adventure Academy Cup for High Flyers. His mum and dad were so proud, they brought the whole flock along to caw and flap him.

Then I gave Yeller his Gold Daring Deed Award for Braveness in a Blizzard. And guess what, the Gold Daring Deed Award for Braveness against Bangs went to L Wolf Esqwire. Also the Silver DD Award for Clues and Courage While Cubnapped went to Master Smellybreff Wolf.

Shame awards do not stop small bruvs being painy and spoilt. He likes pretending to be Uncle Bigbad all the time, so he makes me feed him bakebeans with a shovel or no peace. So today I gave him a good bossabout. I said, "Behave, small bruv! Bakebeans all gone! Now we must buy more! But you have locked up all the gold. If you want bakebeans, just hurry up and remember that combination!"

No good me being Headly, all that did was make him be nasty to get me back. He is hiding somewhere, also he has taken the safe with him. When I catch him I will probly go RAVING MAD at him like Dad.

Yours gggrly,

L

Dear M and D,

I found Smells, he was in the garden with the safe. Plus Mister Twister's leftover rockets. He stuffed all the rockets under the safe and lit them.

Good thing I am a hero about bangs now. Because Smells's 1 went

KERBLAMMM CHINKLE CHINKLE!!

Smells says he only wanted to open the safe for bakebean money. He did not mean to blow small lumps of it all over Frettnin Forest, but a bit late now. It took us all day finding just 2 gold pieces.

Also he has blown his sailor suit off. Plus his tailfur. But do not fear and fret, Stubbs has glued him on some grey tedfluff for now.

Yours with ears dinging,

L

ADVENTURE ACADEMY
FRETTNIN FOREST, BEASTSHIRE
HEADS; LITTLE WOLF AND YELLER WOLF, ESQS

Dear M and D,

Good old Smells, he gave us a BRILLIANT new idea.

We will start up a new scary school for brute beasts. Our teaching will be Hunting and Haunting. We will do Hunting for Gold in the daytime, plus Horror Haunting in the nightime. We will play Hello Ween and have Midnight Feasts of bakebeans (canteen size). *That* will tempt back the ghost of Uncle Bigbad. So then he can teach us Walking Through Walls, Shocking for Beginners, ect. Also Stubbs can teach Spooksuit Making and Flying Lessons.

And Smells can be a small Horror and our new school will be called Haunted Hall, the Spookiest School in the World!!!

Yr xcited
   Little

HAUNTED HALL
FOR SMALL HORRORS

Dear Mum and Dad,

Me, Yeller, Stubbs and Smells are waiting for midnight. We have all got our spooksuits and glowmasks on. Also the bakebeans are going bubblebubble in the pot, hmmm nice. Uncle Bigbad's ghost will appear soonly, then the fun can start!!!

Yours spookingly,
Little

HAUNTED HALL
FOR SMALL HORRORS

Dear Mum and Dad,

   I have filled Yeller's book right up now, so I am going to do LITTLE WOLF'S DIARY OF DARING DEEDS in all different colours on the front of it. That means now I am the bet winner, Yeller owes me 3 trillions of yummy grub! So hurry up Springtime and hurry up parents to come for a nice scary midnight feast. From now on the shocks are on me!

AWHHHHHOOOOOOOOOOOOOOOOOOOOOOOOO!

from

Little Wolf